FINNGLAS OF THE HORSES

When Finn_____ ___ ___er beloved
horse _____ _____ning to travel 'to
t_____

____ ____ __panions, Niall and Pangur
___ __ white cat, Finnglas sets sail in a
__all and leaky coracle for the Hall of
Pillars, the Place of Desire. But that is
only the beginning of a great adventure.

This is the second book about Finnglas
and Pangur Bán, but it can be read on its
own. The first book in the series, *Pangur
Bán, the White Cat*, was shortlisted for
the Guardian Children's Fiction Award,
1984.

Fay Sampson is the author of ten books
for children and teenagers. She lives with
her family in a centuries-old Devon
cottage, overlooking Dartmoor. As well as
writing, she works as a part-time teacher
of mathematics. She spends her holidays
collecting material for her books –
anything from Celtic archaeology on Iona
to whale-watching.

Finnglas of the Horses

FAY SAMPSON

Illustration by Kathy Wyatt

A LION PAPERBACK
Tring · Batavia · Sydney

Copyright © 1985 Fay Sampson

Published by
Lion Publishing plc
Icknield Way, Tring, Herts, England
ISBN 0 85648 899 2
Lion Publishing Corporation
1705 Hubbard Avenue, Batavia, Illinois 60510, USA
ISBN 0 85648 899 2
Albatross Books Pty Ltd
PO Box 320, Sutherland, NSW 2232, Australia
ISBN 0 86760 608 8

First edition 1985
Reprinted 1986
All rights reserved

British Library Cataloguing in Publication Data
Sampson, Fay
  Finnglas of the horses.
  I. Title
  823'.914[J]   PZ7
  ISBN 0 85648 899 2

Printed and bound in Great Britain by
Cox & Wyman Ltd, Reading

To Margaret

1

The Princess Finnglas called down from the roof she was thatching.

'It is finished!'

She tossed her mallet to the tall young monk, Niall.

'There! The abbey my father burned I have rebuilt.'

Pangur, the white cat, climbed up the ladder beside her. He carried in his mouth a garland of leaves and flowers. Laughing, they hung it from the gable-end of the building. From below them a clear voice rang out above the screams of the gulls.

'Let the love of the Dolphin fill this place with his people;
Let the light of the Dolphin shine in the words they will write;
Let the Dolphin's laughter warm their hearts and ours, now and for ever.'

'Amen!' sang Finnglas and Niall and Pangur Bán.

The white-robed Abbess Drusticc was beckoning them down. Already the monks and nuns were walking home from labour, tools hoisted on their shoulders, their voices chanting psalms in the evening air as they came.

The three friends stood together on the grassy ledge. Proudly they looked round them at the refectory, the schoolroom, the sleeping-huts, tucked weather-wise into the nooks and crannies of the cliff. Beside them stood the new-thatched library.

'A year, it has taken. But I have kept my promise,' said Finnglas.

The Abbess watched her keenly.

'So? You'll be wanting to put to sea again, I suppose.'

'*No*! I've come home to stay,' mewed the little white cat,

Pangur Bán. He lifted his face and sniffed the scent of supper drifting along the ledges.

'No!' protested Niall. The young giant of a monk looked down at his hands, coarse and calloused now from hoisting stones. But he was the greatest artist in the abbey. Those hands could copy the flowing words of the Gospels, and fill the spaces with sketches of marvellous beasts, then paint the pages with glowing purple and gold.

'What use is an abbey without monks, or a library without books? My work is here, until I have filled it with riches greater than the treasures King Kernac burned.'

But Finnglas swung round and scanned the western sea.

The harbour was slate-grey in the evening light. Below the abbey, the waves broke white as whey on the dark rocks. But beyond the reefs, the breakers came rolling in from the sunset in endless bars of black and gold and silver.

'It was there. *There,* that I lost her. Where the reefs end and the deep ocean begins. Melisant, the most valiant of horses, that could outrace the chariots of the wind. For love she bore me into the sea, pursuing you. For love she struggled until she could swim no more. For love of me she sank beneath the waves. And not a day has passed but I have sworn that I would set out to find her, once I was free.'

The sea sighed on the shore. Her friends looked at her with worried eyes.

'Finnglas,' Niall told her gently, 'Melisant drowned.'

'She didn't! How dare you say that!' Her eyes were sparkling between anger and tears. 'Is there not a realm of the mermaids under the sea? Have you and I and Pangur Bán not been there? What if she is still alive, still galloping, somewhere in the land beneath the waves? Dishonour to me if I do not rescue her!'

The golden sun was slipping below the ocean. Dark shadows stalked the cliffs.

Drusticc wiped her hands on her apron and packed the tools away in their leather satchel.

'Suppertime. We have all known loss and sorrow. Your father is grieving still in the Summer Isle, west of the sunset.

He thinks his daughter is dead. It is home you should be going, Finnglas Red-Hand.'

Finnglas spun round on her. 'No father of mine is Kernac the king! Have I not been a year rebuilding what he has burned? It is my brave horse Melisant I go to find.'

'Melisant is dead,' repeated Niall. 'You cannot bring her back. Once, in a moment's anger, I killed your brother. And bitterly this abbey suffered for it. But only Arthmael the Dolphin can undo what we have done.'

The princess stared up into the young monk's face.

'Tell me this, Niall. Did you love my brother Martin, whom you slew?'

Niall's voice came low through the twilight.

'I have chosen to be a monk. It is not likely I shall ever have a son. You know I loved your brother dearly.'

'And I loved Melisant, and I have lost her. If you will not come with me, I shall seek her alone.'

The evening wind whispered in the new-thatched eaves. The scent of supper drifted down from the kitchen. Behind them, the library stood empty.

'Oh . . . *Sprats*!' wailed Pangur.

And after that, there was nothing more to be said.

'It's a very *small* boat,' said Pangur. 'And it's seen good service.'

Niall bent over and touched the bottom of the coracle. It was a tiny, round boat without a sail. The leather had been holed and patched.

'This is all I can spare you,' said Drusticc. 'It is few enough boats that King Kernac's raiders left us. And there are many hungry mouths to feed from the fishing.'

The monks had laid a skin of water in the boat, a sack of oats and a new pair of oars, white and slender, cut from straight-grained ash.

'There's no sail,' said Niall.

'It has oars,' Finnglas said defiantly. 'We can choose our own way.'

They knelt on the beach before Drusticc. She laid her hand on each of their heads in turn.

'The arms of the Father cradle you on his ocean.
The eye of the Son steer you under his stars.
And the wind of the Spirit bring you at the last to the hearth that is home and the blood of your belonging.'

They launched the coracle on the morning tide.

There were feathers of mist on the water, moving over the surface like ghostly birds. Long before they passed beyond the reefs, the wool-clad crowd of nuns and monks on the beach had dimmed into the distance like a flock of sheep, and their calls of farewell had faded in the fog like the cries of curlews.

The grey-green water slid against the rocks without spray, without noise. The last reef melted behind them in the mist. They were alone on the ocean now.

'It must have been here,' said Finnglas.

Niall stopped rowing.

'What are you going to do?' asked Pangur.

For answer, Finnglas unfastened her chequered cloak and let it fall. She dived from the boat, sending it rocking wildly. Niall and Pangur grabbed at the sides and looked at each other in alarm. They counted the slowly passing heartbeats. They had reached fifty before she surfaced beside them, spluttering, like a wet seal. She looked at them crossly, without speaking, then took a deep breath and dived again.

Long, silent moments passed. Then her head broke surface again, further from the boat, dark and dripping in the mist. Niall rowed towards her. She gasped for air, her arms outspread on the water. But before they could reach her, she dived for the third time and disappeared.

Now time lengthened in unbroken silence. Pangur began to lean over the side, peering down through the cloudy green water. At last Niall's hands went to the girdle that fastened his robe. As the knot fell free, two small hands shot skywards. A thatch of wet brown hair followed, a red, choking face. Silently they pulled her aboard and wrapped the thick cloak round her.

'Well, what did you expect?' asked Niall. 'It is a year since she went from us.'

'I couldn't breathe! I couldn't see! I thought I could go down to the land of the mermaids and journey there till I found her. But it's not the same. The way was closed to me.'

Pangur looked back into the depths, remembering.

'Arthmael had broken the spell of the mermaids in the great Undoing. Their magic does not rule the water now.'

'I'm not so sure,' said Niall, suddenly gripping the oars. 'Listen!'

Out of the mist a distant note of music called, high and haunting. Now it was coming nearer, rising on the swell, clearer, sweeter, eddying round them in the fog, its echoes teasing them.

'That is very like a mermaid's song,' murmured Niall.

They looked at each other doubtfully.

11

'Where is she?' growled Pangur.

They searched nervously all round the boat, even under the sea. The air was rocked with singing. But still they could see nothing.

Then the coracle tilted suddenly and spun round. White fingers grasped the gunwale. A fair face appeared, mantled with long gold hair beaded with dewdrops. Eyes green as spring-time turf smiled up at them.

There was a frightened silence. Niall's face went white. The hairs on Pangur's neck were bristling.

'Morwenna!' whispered Finnglas.

A year ago, they had heard her song break as she cradled Arthmael's body in her arms and died beside him.

The mermaid threw back her hair and laughed at them.

'Yes! Don't look so afraid! Why are your faces so pale?'

'But you were . . . We thought . . . '

She let go of the boat, spinning it wildly in her merriment.

'That I was a ghost! Is *that* what you thought? Some sad and fearful shadow from the past? Oh, Niall! Oh, Finnglas! Oh, Pangur Bán! Don't you understand? It is those who have danced with the Dolphin who are truly alive!'

Tears of laughter were flashing in her eyes.

'Morwenna!' Niall gave a great shout of joy. 'Then it's really you!'

'Look! Is this what you think death is?'

She shimmered beneath the boat in a flash of blue like a diving kingfisher. She shot through the swell on the other side, breaking the still water into a thousand leaping circles. They glimpsed her gold hair streaming through the flying spray. Swiftly, joyfully she danced in spirals round them, sending the coracle rocking giddily.

Then she swam back to them and lay still in the water, looking up at them more thoughtfully.

'I felt your need. Someone called from under the water. You are very wet, Finnglas. Is something wrong?'

'Yes,' Finnglas spoke with difficulty. 'It is Melisant, my horse. I lost her below the waves. Oh, tell me, Morwenna! When you swam in Ancofva, in the halls of the mermaids, did you ever see a piebald pony, with a white blaze on her nose?'

Morwenna shook her head slowly.

'No. And well I remember that day. You three were the last creatures from Earth to follow the mermaids' call. And then the Dolphin came, and I danced with him to death and beyond. Since then, I have not returned to the halls of bewitchment, to Ancofva, the Place of Forgetting.'

'Then you cannot help? You cannot tell me where she might be?' There were tears in Finnglas's eyes.

Morwenna thought for a long moment. Then she slipped beneath the swell. For a while they did not see her. When she rose again, she looked searchingly into all their faces.

'This much I know. But the knowing of it may be dangerous. In Ancofva they sang a song of Hyreth. In the Place of Forgetting they sang of the Land of Desire. They say that in Hyreth, in the Hall of the Pillars, all those who come shall be granted their heart's desire.'

'Then I could ask for Melisant's life? I want to bring her back more than anything in the world!'

Morwenna gazed steadily up at the princess.

'More than anything, Finnglas?'

'Are you doubting my word?'

'It shall be well for you, if you speak true. You may claim your heart's desire. But beware. If you have spoken falsely, the thing that you choose will have the power to destroy you.'

'The Princess Finnglas does not lie! It is Melisant's life I seek before anything else! By my own fault I lost her. By myself I shall bring her back.'

The green eyes held hers silently. Then the mermaid turned to the others.

'And what of you two?'

Niall and Pangur looked at each other and nodded.

'We did a great wrong to Finnglas. Her choice is ours. We will ask for Melisant's life.'

'Is that truly your heart's desire, Niall? More than the most beautiful things the world can offer?'

'It is,' Niall said.

'And mine,' said Pangur.

The mermaid's lips curved in a smile. 'Is it so, Pangur? That, even more than the love of food?'

'Finnglas has chosen. We follow her to the death,' said Pangur, and at once he wished he hadn't.

With a sparkle of old mischief in her eyes, the mermaid spun round laughing.

'To the death, is it, Pangur? Then hold to what you have sworn, and to each other, or you stand in great danger. To the north, and follow me to Hyreth! You shall have your heart's desire, if your hearts are true.'

And she dived away into the mist.

3

'Forty days rowing,' said Pangur. 'Where is she taking us?'

'To Melisant,' said Finnglas firmly.

'Or death?'

'I don't care what it is,' declared Niall, 'if only I can stand on dry land again. Look at my hands. They've got blisters on them as big as dinner-plates. I'll never be able to hold a paintbrush again.'

'I hardened mine on Melisant's reins,' said Finnglas. 'These are warrior's hands. They were trained to gallop a horse and wield a sword.'

'But I was a painter,' said Niall sadly. 'All my skill was in the making of beautiful books.'

Pangur said nothing. He was only the convent cat.

Still Morwenna swam on, while Finnglas and Niall took turns at rowing. They followed her dancing in the daylight, her singing in the darkness. Only when they rested, exhausted, did she turn her flower-face towards them, her green eyes deeply thoughtful.

But there came a dawn when Pangur stiffened and gasped.

'There! You've got your wish, Niall!'

The sun leaped up behind them. The little coracle came rocking out of the mist into a summer morning and a sunlit isle. High on a hill a whitewashed palace blazed.

Niall stopped rowing. They all stared at the island.

'Go on! Go on!' cried Finnglas. 'I shall find her here!'

'And what else besides?' asked Niall.

The bay was silent. There was only the creak and splash of oars through the silk-smooth water. A meadow ran down from the palace to the shore. Nothing stirred upon it. There were no horses grazing. Even the ripples hardly sighed upon the sand.

They touched the beach. Morwenna came gliding up to them. Her eyes were troubled, deep green as shadowed moss.

'I cannot take you further. And my heart is heavy that I have brought you here. Behold the Island of Hyreth, the Place of Desire.'

'I don't like it,' said Pangur. 'Can't we go home?'

'It's a fine palace,' Niall said, trying to sound braver than he felt. 'Fit for a king.'

'And I'm a king's daughter,' said Finnglas. 'I'm not afraid.' She walked ahead up the beach.

Morwenna's voice came singing after them.

'Be sure that your hearts are true to what you have sworn. Beware! Beware your desires!'

But Finnglas strode on through the meadow, with the buttercups brushing her boots.

They climbed the hill. No cattle moved on its slopes. The palace rose above them. The wall glistened in the sun, new-washed with lime. Its roof shone golden with fresh thatch. But it was utterly still. No smoke rose from its roof. The doors and windows stood open, but no one came and went.

'If you're a king's daughter,' muttered Niall, 'you tell me this. In your father's dun, don't you have warriors guarding the gate? Fires in the kitchen? Slaves working in the fields? Where is everybody?'

'Let's go back,' said Pangur. 'It's dangerous.'

He looked over his shoulder at the glittering sea stretching away to the horizon. For a moment his eyes searched it hungrily, longing to see a burst of white spray and a leaping back. But the waves rose and fell without sign of life. Only a patch of periwinkle beside the coracle showed where Morwenna watched.

Finnglas tossed her head. 'If you're afraid, you can both go back. This quest is mine. I can brave it alone.'

And she walked through the silent gate into the yard.

Not a mastiff barked, nor a voice challenged her. A dark doorway stood open in front of them. Over it twined a pattern of flowers and serpents, from which the wise might disentangle a chain of words.

'What does it say?' asked Finnglas. 'I can't read it.'

Niall shaded his eyes.

'Nor can I. It is an older script than we write in the abbey.
I like it not.'

'I'm going in,' said Finnglas. And she disappeared into
the shadows.

Niall looked at Pangur and spread his hands helplessly.

'I can't let her go alone.' The skirt of his robe vanished
into the gloom.

Pangur was left trembling on the threshold. He looked
from the dark doorway to the sunlit sea.

'Oh . . . *Elvers*!' he wailed, and scuttled in after the others.

4

Pangur stopped short, eyes widening in the shadows, nostrils unbearably stretched. In the centre of the hall was a table, loaded with food. Bowls of fresh milk, golden with cream. Bread still steaming with the fragrance of baking. Legs of pork. Fish wrapped in leaves. Pitchers of ale. Three stools were set. Three plates of solid gold. The head of the table was empty.

All round it the floor was strewn with fresh straw, loosely-lying, as though no foot had stepped on it.

They stood, torn with indecision. Hunger was leaping in their throats, a ravening wolf, after weeks of cold water and oats in the coracle. But fear, like a fire in the thatch, seemed to crackle in the stillness all around them. It was hard not to run. And yet the food . . .

'Milk! Fresh milk!' cried Pangur, and leaped on to the table.

Niall's hand smacked down and knocked him to the floor.

'No! Don't touch it! It's magic! . . . I'm sorry, Pangur. But this is fairy food. And those who eat what the fair folk have bewitched are never satisfied with wholesome food again. That milk has the power to destroy you.'

Pangur shivered, feeling his tail stiffen and the skin creep along his back.

But Finnglas turned away impatiently.

'It was not food we came seeking, but Melisant.' She laid her hand on the table and her voice rang through the dark hall. 'Where are you who set this table for us? We are three travellers and we come to claim our heart's desire. Dishonour to you if you do not grant it to us.'

The rafters gave back her voice unanswered. Finnglas's face fell as her hope drained away.

'Is there no one here?'

'In the Hall of the Pillars?' murmured Niall, looking round him.

But this room held only the loaded table.

Finnglas moved restlessly away to the dark walls. She found a latch. The door opened on a sleeping chamber, silent, empty. The next room was the same, fresh-swept, but deserted. And the next. And the next. She moved to the fifth door and flung it open. The others held their breath. But the last chamber was empty too. Outside, there was utter silence.

'That's that, then,' said Niall with a sigh of relief.

He moved towards the courtyard. Pangur followed. But Finnglas stood obstinately in the middle of the hall. A tear began to creep down her cheek.

'Oh, where *is* she?'

Pangur turned on the threshold.

'Finnglas?'

And then he saw. Behind Finnglas. Where the light from the open doorway fell on the opposite wall, a tiny door, too small for anyone but a cat to enter without bending. Tall Finnglas had walked straight past it.

Pangur edged further away. Just behind him was sunshine and safety. No one else had seen that little door. If he did not say anything, they could all go back to the coracle and Morwenna and home. No one need ever know what he had seen.

And then he saw Finnglas's face.

'Miaow!' he said, and he walked past her to the tiny door and pushed it open.

He gasped, and halted. Light blinded him. The others came crawling after him and took a step into the room before they stopped. The chamber was flooded with light from sky-filled windows. The walls blazed with gold.

Golden cloaks, thick, crusted, quilted, embroidered. Cloth of gold, gold clasps, gold borders, tasselled gold, twisted gold, golden silk, golden thread, gold leaf. Heavy, rich, royal, gold for a ransom, hung along one wall. Twelve cloaks of gold.

On another, golden swords. Hilts of gold, shafts of gold, filigree, twisted, dipped, solid, pointed, coiling, polished, bossed, all gold, gold from their pommels down to the tracery on their long steel blades. Gold on the scabbards, jewels on golden scabbards. Twelve gold swords in twelve gold scabbards.

And on the third, collars of gold. Torques, pendants, necklaces, rings, ropes, studded, jewelled, rounded, mounted, polished, shining, twining, gleaming, glistening, magical gold. Twelve golden collars.

A feast for the eyes, more than the feast of food. Making its own hunger. Blinding the heart. Making the eyes shine and the fingers itch and the feet begin to move.

Finnglas hasting to those swords like a swallow to her young. To be equipped as a warrior once more.

'The swords!'

Small hands went reaching out.

'The cloaks! The embroidery! Look at that cloth!'

With a glance of disgust at his worn and dirty robe, Niall was running across the room, his arms stretched out, his artist's fingers yearning to feel that marvellous workmanship.

Pangur eyed the golden collars. He knew what they meant. Those rich, round links of gold. If Pangur Bán wore such a collar round his neck . . . The royal badge of kingship.

Tempted, he was moving slowly towards it. Then,

'MIAOW!'

His scream of warning split the others' dreams. Finnglas and Niall whirled round. Pangur was bristling in the centre of the room.

Before him, unregarded till now, stood four stone pillars, carved with the symbols of an older power. The stag, the serpent, the wolf, the bear. And on the fifth, the head of a horned man with staring eyes.

Pangur's bright green gaze was fixed on this central pillar, his back arched, fur spiky with fear, tail stiff as a pine branch, ears flattened against his head. On its marble top sat a golden cat, still as a statue. It had been watching them.

Pangur began to stalk around the pillar. The golden cat turned slowly, following with its red-gold eyes.

'Is it an enemy?' called Finnglas.

'Yes!' whined Pangur, every muscle tense.

'We could just go,' Niall said hastily. 'We haven't touched anything.'

'Not yet!' said Finnglas. 'Not till I have this!'

Her two hands flew out to the nearest sword. A great pommel of round, red gold, laced with gilt wire. Her hands were hungry for a weapon. They started to close. The eyes of the golden cat widened, glowing.

'*Don't touch it*!' yelled Pangur.

The yellow cat leaped to another pillar and whirled round, spitting at Pangur.

But Finnglas was not to be forbidden. Niall and Pangur watched her eyes lock with the cat's in a battle of wills. Stiff as a temple carving, the golden cat stood poised on amber feet, staring at Finnglas with the stillness of hate. Her hand was moving imperceptibly behind her, reaching out, nearer and nearer, towards the golden sword. The golden cat's eyes grew wide again, brilliant. Finnglas's fingers were close against the wall. The cat's body seemed to swell, to glow with triumph.

'*Finnglas! No*!' shrieked Pangur, and hurled himself on to her shoulders, clinging, dragging, clawing her sideways.

As she tumbled off balance, her outstretched hand caught the hilt of the sword and knocked it from the wall. There was a great flash of flame, a roar like thunder. The palace shook to its foundations. Finnglas and Pangur disappeared in a pall of smoke.

With a screech of rage, the golden cat jumped out through the window.

There was a smell of singed fur. Finnglas had screamed with pain. Niall dived through the smoke where they had been.

The murk cleared slowly. He came face to face with Finnglas. On the floor beside her lay the gold-hilted sword. And the whole white wall behind them, where it had fallen, was cracked with a huge brown scorchmark. It had singed Pangur's tail. Finnglas was nursing a great burn on her hand, wrapping it in a sooty fold of her cloak.

'Finnglas!' cried Niall, 'Are you badly hurt? There are tears in your eyes.'

She lifted her stricken face to him.

'You think the Princess Finnglas weeps for pain? Don't you understand? Don't you see what I have done? In the Hall of the Pillars I was offered my heart's desire. And instead of Melisant's life I chose a sword!'

Smoke drifted past them through the window and curled above the roof. From the beach they heard Morwenna's anxious cry.

5

The three of them stood in a long, bitter silence. Niall hung his head.

'I am as bad as you. For love of a painted page I once killed your brother. Yet still I put beauty higher than our friendship. I would have taken a cloak. It was only Pangur who saved you.'

'But I wanted a royal collar,' Pangur confessed. 'Can you think of anything so silly? Me, a king!'

And the tip of his nose went pink with shame.

'But we didn't take anything. Pangur stopped us in time. We can still claim our wish.'

The cracked wall behind her began to creak. Fragments of plaster dropped to the floor.

'It's too late,' said Niall. 'We had our chance.'

They scrambled out of the hall and crossed the sunlit courtyard. But halfway to the gate, Finnglas stopped suddenly.

'What a fool I am! The stables! I forgot the stables! Where else should I look for a horse?'

And she was running away from them, her leather boots thudding across the yard. Pangur started after her, but Niall stayed him.

'She has to learn. What we have done, is done. Let her go alone.'

She vanished into the shadows, while they waited in the sleeping sun-drenched silence. Smoke rose from the blackened thatch. The lime-washed walls were netted with tiny cracks.

'Niall! Finnglas! Pangur Bán!'

'It's Morwenna. She saw the firebolt strike the palace. She's afraid for our lives.'

The sunlight fell brilliantly upon the whitewashed ramparts. The ground beneath their feet began to tremble slightly. Still Finnglas did not come.

'She's been gone a long time,' said Pangur. '*Finnglas*?'

His call died away in the silence. At last they went anxiously to the stables and looked in. Fresh straw littered the earthen floor. New halters hung from the wall posts. The stalls were empty. At the far end Finnglas was leaning against the wall, weeping bitterly into the crook of her arm.

They came slowly towards her. They could not think what to say to comfort her.

'I almost found her! Just for a moment, as I came through the door, I thought I heard her whinny; I thought I caught that breath of sweat and horsehair. And then it was gone, and there was nothing here. Oh, Melisant, Melisant! Why did I ever forget you? I have turned my back on you a second time!'

Niall laid his hand on her shoulder. Pangur rubbed his warm fur round her legs.

'Come, Finnglas. It is time to be going. I don't like it here.'

And as he spoke, there came a long shuddering roar from the palace. They ran to the door. The glittering, new-thatched, new-washed hall quivered, caved, crumbled, crashed earthwards. A pall of smoke and dust rose like a fog. From the sea came a frightened shriek.

They looked at each other, white-faced.

Niall said softly, 'If we had taken the sword . . . the cloak . . . the collar . . . '

They stared at the smoking ruin. There was a taste of dust and ashes in their mouths.

Again the cry rose from the beach.

'Niall? Why don't you answer? Are you safe?'

Niall started to run. But the mermaid's call broke off suddenly. They heard a startled shriek, and then a peal of laughter.

'What is happening?'

'Morwenna is laughing!'

And all at once they swung round to each other, hope shining in all their faces.

'It is *him*!'

'He has come back!'

'It must be Arthmael!'

And at that name they went racing for the gate, flying down the hillside, bounding over the buttercups and daisies, with Pangur on small white legs out in front of the others. And out on the bay he saw what he had been longing to see.

The water splintered into diamonds. The curving, leaping, plunging, soaring grace of the Dolphin silvered air and sea. He flung himself between depths and earth and sky, and as he danced, his black tail twined around the blue of Morwenna's, so that the two of them were like night and day, sporting with the stars and the sun in their eyes.

Finnglas, Niall and Pangur rushed down to the shore, but at the edge of the beach they found their steps slowing. A shyness came over them as they crossed the sand. They stopped at the tideline.

Arthmael swam into the shallows. One bright eye sparkled up at them.

'Well?'

His voice was high and full of laughter. But though he was smiling, they found they could not meet that eye.

Finnglas stared down at her boots. She burst out,

'I'm sorry! I could have saved her life, but I chose a sword. Oh, Arthmael, I'm sorry!'

'And so am I.'

'And I,' murmured Niall and Pangur.

The great dolphin rushed up through the water and balanced on his tail. His cool beak stroked the blisters on Finnglas's palm. He drew her pain into himself.

'What is done, is done, Finnglas. The hand will heal. But the heart remembers,' he said very gently.

She cried out. 'Oh, Arthmael, what does it mean? Have I lost her for ever? Tell me what I must do to rescue her now.'

Arthmael turned a somersault and came back to her. Both bright eyes watched her now.

'How far would you venture to save what is lost, Finnglas?'

'To the world's end!'

'Finnglas!' said Niall.

'Miaow!' warned Pangur.

The grin broadened on Arthmael's face.

'*Well*, Finnglas?'

The princess reddened and hung her head.

'I will *try* to follow, whatever you say, Arthmael.'

'Then be a fool, Finnglas, and come with me. I cannot tell if at the world's end you will find what you need. But I know that what you will find there has need of *you*.'

And the white wake of his fin shot like an arrow into the north and disappeared.

'What did he mean?' cried Pangur. 'Where has he gone?'

But Morwenna was already turning in a sparkle of blue.

Finnglas grabbed the boat. 'Quick! After him! Wherever Arthmael goes we must follow him!'

6

They grew lean and hard on that voyage. The oars strained their arms. The sun burned their skin. The sack of oats grew small and thin. Still Arthmael rushed them northwards, with Morwenna racing beside him as though she felt his urgency.

When they saw land at last, it was low and barren under a hard, blue sky. Niall rowed nearer over the glassy sea. Finnglas grasped the bows, staring forward.

Grey rock rose out of the sea like a crusted whale. No grass greened its humped back. Even the shore was bare of seaweed. A cloud of quarrelling black-backed gulls fought over it.

Arthmael slowed, and rolled his head towards the coracle.

'It is not *quite* the end of the world, Finnglas. But it is far enough.'

'What place is this?' asked Morwenna. 'I have never heard tell of it.'

He turned his grave smile upon her.

'No. In Ancofva of the Mermaids, in the Place of Forgetting, how should they sing of Gwanegreth the Forgotten?'

Gwanegreth. The name fell sadly on the ear.

Pangur growled. 'No watering place here, by the look of it. I never saw an island so dead. Nothing but gulls.'

Finnglas stiffened suddenly. 'No! There is something else. Look!'

There were black shadows under the grey rocks. Patches of white between the boulders. Sometimes the shadows and the patches moved. As the coracle glided closer, the shifting shapes began to herd together into a stream, a slow-pouring river, trickling down the gulleys to the shore.

Finnglas drew her breath in a great shaking gasp and flung

her arms around Pangur.

'*Horses*! Oh, blessed Arthmael! There are *horses*! I shall find her here! . . . Melisant! Wait for me! I'm coming!'

And she leaped over the bows into the clear green water. Niall hurriedly shipped the oars.

'Wait!' Arthmael commanded. 'You will be needed soon enough.'

They watched her splash through the low surf.

The tide of horses darkened the shore as they flooded slowly out of the gulleys towards her. Through the glittering air her eyes raked the herd. Bay, brown, grey, piebald. They saw her brush the water from her eyes, trying to separate one pony from another, searching desperately for that one white blaze on a jet-black muzzle.

'Melisant?' her voice called hopefully. 'Melisant?'

The ponies were stumbling over the stones so slowly. The sea dragged at her boots as she waded ashore.

Now she could see them more clearly. The breath caught in her throat. A sorry procession was staggering down the beach to meet her. Feeble-legged ponies, limping, their long heads hanging in distress. Chestnut, skewbald, dappled, black. With staring coats and swollen knees. Ribs starkly showing, stomachs distended, eyes almost too dull and heavy to lift with hope as they pleaded for help. Some of them fell even before they could reach her.

Her wild shriek struck the cliffs. Niall was over the side in an instant, with Pangur clinging to his shoulder. Finnglas stood trembling, hearing the echo of that terrible cry and knowing it for her own voice.

A white stallion nuzzled dry lips against her cheek.

'Food!' he croaked.

A hand closed over hers. Niall was beside her.

'Niall!' she cried out to him. 'The ponies! Look at them!'

'They're starving,' he said slowly, scanning the bleached, bare rocks. 'It hasn't rained. They've eaten every blade of grass. They've even stripped the seaweed off the beach. There's nothing left.'

She broke away from him then and shouldered her way

28

wildly through the herd, searching, searching. Her lips moved over and over with Melisant's name. The ponies staggered as she pushed past them. A little bay mare blocked her path.

'Hay!' she murmured. 'For the love of heaven, feed us.'

'Out of my way! It's not you I am seeking.'

Finnglas thrust her aside and stumbled over something just beyond. She stopped short. At her feet, a foal, thin as a skeleton, lay on the shingle with open, lifeless eyes. The bay mare hung her head. Her tongue feebly licked the dead foal.

With a sob, Finnglas turned. She looked round at the pathetic herd, as though she were seeing them all for the first time. They stood where she had pushed them aside, heads drooping. Yet still their listless eyes followed her, their flickering hope not quite extinguished yet. Finnglas reached out her arms to them.

'Forgive me!' she cried. 'Oh, please, forgive me!'

Next moment she was in among them, stroking their noses, running her hands gently over their painful sides, lifting their manes from heavy eyes. She felt their hot breath all around her, their questing mouths nuzzling her empty hands. At last she came face to face with the white stallion. She threw her arms round his neck and buried her head in his mane, weeping as though her heart would break.

Niall's arm came round her shoulder.

'Melisant?' he asked gently.

'She isn't here.' Her voice was muffled.

'Would you wish her here?' asked Niall. 'These ponies are dying.'

'No,' she whispered. 'Oh, Niall, what are we going to do?'

'Ask,' said a small voice at her feet.

They looked down at Pangur. His pointed face was wise and full of importance.

'Expect,' he added.

A dawn of hope broke over Finnglas's face. She went bounding over the shingle down to the sea.

'Arthmael! Arthmael!' she cried.

The slow swell broke into sparkling spray as the dolphin leaped out of the water.

'Did somebody call me?'

Morwenna came swimming in beside him, lifting her flower-face from the waves, listening. Finnglas called across the water to them.

'Arthmael! You've got to help us! The ponies. They're dying of hunger. You've got to do something!'

The dolphin turned a somersault over Morwenna and stopped in front of Finnglas. His bright eyes watched her curiously.

'What?'

'Feed them! You can do it, can't you? Oh, please, I know you can!'

Arthmael raced away, stood on his tail, danced over six waves and came back to Finnglas.

'*You* feed them,' he said, and disappeared with a splash.

Finnglas spat the foam from her face and stamped her foot. 'Oh, don't be silly, Arthmael! We can't. You know we can't. We haven't got corn.'

Niall called across. 'Oh, yes, we have. There are still a few oats in the coracle.'

'But that was hardly enough for the three of us. It won't save a hundred horses. We need a whole shipful!'

Arthmael's beak flipped Finnglas into the air. She fell into the water with a cry and a splash.

'Then *get* a shipful,' said Arthmael reprovingly. 'Don't look at me. I'm a dolphin, not a cargo vessel. And what are you sitting in the water for? You look ridiculous.'

Niall strode down to the water's edge and helped Finnglas up.

'We could do it!' His eyes were eager. 'What are a few more blisters when we've come so far? We've got a boat, we've got oars, haven't we? We can row away as fast as they will take us. We can find the nearest land, buy hay and corn, row back again.'

'Brave Niall!' cried Arthmael approvingly. 'Why do you think I brought you here?'

'But there isn't *time*,' cried Finnglas. 'They'll be dead by then.'

Arthmael swam a circle round her.

'*All* of them, Finnglas?' he asked gently.

Niall was already splashing back to the coracle. He laid the thin sack of oats over his shoulder and trudged with it through the surf and up the beach. With shuffling eagerness the ponies came pressing down around him. He pushed them off gently and began to open the bag. The stallion nuzzled his hand hopefully. One by one he fed them a palmful of food.

Too soon it was all gone.

'There. I have given you everything we had.'

'Now there's nothing left for us,' Pangur mewed anxiously. 'What are we going to eat? How are we going to pay for the corn when we find it? And what are we going to carry it back in? There's hardly room for three of us in the coracle, let alone food for a hundred horses!'

'Ask?' Arthmael teased him. 'Expect?'

Then the dolphin gazed steadily at the princess.

'Well, Finnglas? How far will you go now to save Melisant?'

'She isn't here,' said Finnglas in a low voice. 'You know she isn't.'

'Oh, but she is! Look behind you.'

Finnglas whirled round, her eyes shining. The little bay mare whinnied softly and nudged her hand. Finnglas's face fell cruelly.

'That isn't her. Don't be a fool, Arthmael!'

'I am the world's fool.'

He flicked a great burst of water into the air. The glistening drops rained down on the hanging heads of the horses, like a baptism. 'They called to me out of their great need. And so I name them Melisant. And Melisant. And Melisant . . . *Now* do you see? They are all Melisant. And only you can save them. Be a fool, Finnglas.'

She stared at him for a long moment. Then she wiped the tears from her cheeks and drew herself up proudly.

'I was a king's daughter once. I said to my slave, "Do this", and she did it. And to a warrior, "Go", and he went. Whatever you command me, I will do.'

And she waded out to the coracle.

Arthmael danced round her joyfully.

'Now you speak not like a princess but a true queen.'

He dived through her legs and tumbled her into the coracle. 'Well, don't just sit there! Make all the haste you can. Many lives lie in your hands. May the wind of God be behind you, and the courage of fools in your hearts!'

He turned, and stroked Morwenna's side lovingly.

'And you. Do now what you were made to do. Sing. While we are gone, sing with all the magic of your being. Sing to the dying the song that holds back the dark.'

As Niall heaved the boat across the swell, Morwenna's song began to rise behind them. Borne across the wind like an embroidered banner, spreading to the sky, quickening the blood, lifting the heart with hope. Small, brave, and beautiful. Long after the waves hid Gwanegreth, they heard Morwenna singing to the horses.

8

Niall's shoulders bent strongly to the oars. The coracle laboured on, still heading north.

'It's getting misty,' said Finnglas. 'I've lost sight of Arthmael.'

'I still don't know what he expects us to do,' grumbled Pangur. 'How can we carry corn in this coracle?'

'Listen,' said Finnglas.

Niall stopped rowing and peered anxiously over his shoulder into the gloom. Through the thick twilight they heard the whisper of waves on wood and the creak of ropes.

'It sounds like a ship. I don't feel safe in this coracle. Ahoy there!'

His voice echoed dully back to him out of the mist. There was no answering cry.

'Look,' hissed Pangur. 'On the starboard bow.' The hair on his neck was standing upright.

A great, grey wall came looming across their bows, gliding over the sullen, sucking sea. The sails flapped lifeless. The rigging hung slack. The decks were dead.

Only one rope ran taut from the carved prow down into the sea.

'There's something towing it,' murmured Pangur.

A sleek black head rolled out of the swell and dipped again.

'Arthmael,' said Finnglas in relief. 'We should have known.'

His eye appeared and looked at her challengingly.

'Well, go on! Take it,' he said through a mouthful of wet rope.

She grasped the tow-rope doubtfully.

'Is it for us?'

Arthmael, released, leaped over the coracle, showering them all.

'You need it, don't you? I heard you complaining. Take what the sea offers, and be thankful . . . while you can!'

And he vanished laughing beneath the waves.

Finnglas hauled in the hawser. The little coracle swam closer under the stem. They were in the dark, lapping shadow of a great, planked ship.

'I don't like this,' said Niall. 'Do you think it's safe?'

'If it's a gift from Arthmael, almost certainly not,' Pangur told him. 'But it may be necessary.'

'I'll go first,' Finnglas declared. 'I'm not afraid.'

She swarmed up the rope. There was no sound. The others followed cautiously.

Fog hid the masthead. Water dripped from the rigging, tapping a soft, slow rhythm on the deck. They listened for sudden footsteps or a cry of alarm. There was nothing.

Niall examined his palms. He dried the salt-caked blisters on his robe. Then he peered up at the dim mast and the loose grey rigging.

'I was getting quite good at this a year ago. Before I wrecked the curragh following mermaids. Let's see what we can do.'

Together they set the sails and hauled in the sheets. But they flapped wet and useless in the fog. Finnglas heaved the long, cold tiller across. The ship swung idly.

'We're drifting,' said Pangur. 'It was quicker rowing.'

'Whistle the wind,' suggested Niall.

Finnglas pursed her lips. The thin, sharp sound floated away unanswered. An hour passed. No breeze lifted the sail.

Finnglas stamped her foot. 'Why did he bring such a useless thing? There's no time to waste. The horses are dying *now*!'

Pangur paced along the deck. He sprang up on to the carved prow. His paws expected wood, but he felt cold metal. It was sharp-edged, with the semblance of rough hair. He found himself standing between two large pricked ears. Beyond was a long grey snout and open jaws. In the first

34

startled moment, he wanted to leap down and hide. But it was only a figurehead, swaying in the deepening gloom.

In a sudden fury of impatience, he dug his claws into the wolf-head and snarled. 'Oh, *run*, can't you? Carry us to where the barns are full of corn!'

The jaws growled. A long shudder ran through the ship, tumbling him on to the deck. There was a loud cry from Finnglas.

'I can't hold the tiller!'

The rigging cracked. Niall ran to loosen the sheets as the yard-arm swung across. He quickly cleated it and the sail bellied. The ship swooped forward into the dusk.

Niall came back to the stern. He was shaking all over.

'What did that? What's happening?'

'I don't know. There was a sudden wind. I can't steer the ship. She seems to have a mind of her own.'

Pangur crept back to the stern and rubbed round their legs.

'I think I must have done it. I told the figurehead to find corn, and it took off like a bolting chariot. I don't like it! What ship is this? *Whose* ship is this?'

'It's taking us where we want to go,' said Finnglas.

'Is it? How do we know where it is going?'

They turned in silence and watched the tiller follow the questing snout. The ship loped forward over the darkening sea.

'It doesn't *feel* right,' said Niall. 'There's something strange about this ship. It doesn't smell of wood and hemp and leather.'

'It was Arthmael's gift,' said Finnglas.

They kept close together for comfort through the night. Niall woke first. He rose with a shout.

'Gold! It's all solid gold!'

Pangur's eyes flew open. The ship glistered in the dissolving mist. Gold sheathed the mast and roofed the cabin. Shimmering gold sails filled with the freshening breeze. Sheets of gold silk ran taut round cleats of gold. And high on the prow a rearing golden wolf-head opened its jaws to reveal a scarlet tongue. Inside the cabin, golden goblets stood ready to receive rich wine and golden platters were heaped with salt meat and bread.

Every hair on Pangur's skin was bristling. His eyes were wide with shock. Niall crossed himself.

'What are we doing on a ship like this? Where has it come from?'

Even Finnglas was pale. But she spoke bravely.

'I'm not afraid. It is a royal ship. And I'm a king's daughter.'

'If you're a king's daughter, you tell me this. What is a royal ship doing adrift in the middle of the ocean, without captain or crew? How did Arthmael get it?'

'*Why* did Arthmael get it? Where *is* Arthmael? Oh, I wish he would come.' Pangur searched the dancing sea.

'It doesn't matter. We don't need to know,' said Finnglas firmly. 'It is enough that he has given us what we asked for. Fast sails to catch the wind. A hold that will carry a thousand sacks of corn. And all the gold we could want to buy it with.'

'But is it ours to take?' muttered Niall. 'I don't like it. I'm a simple monk. There's too much power here for me.'

'We must use all the power we can get,' said Finnglas. 'Only we can save the horses.'

'Arthmael said, "Take what the sea gives and be thankful . . . *while you can*",' quoted Pangur. 'I don't like the sound of that.'

'Then don't think of yourself. Think only of the horses.' Finnglas laid her hand on the glittering tiller and felt it move strongly out of her grasp. Her glance flew to the masthead. 'The ship is turning east.'

Niall pushed back his sleeves.

'Come on, Pangur. We took a life once. Now it is time to save others. You and I can set a better sail than that. But I hope to heaven Arthmael knows what he's doing.'

'I'm sure he does,' declared Pangur. 'That's what frightens me!'

9

The wolf-head knew its own way. But they wasted no time.
Day and night, Finnglas and Niall's hands were busy on the
ropes, spreading the sails, catching every shift of wind, racing
for the east. The days shortened, the wind blew colder and
a thin veil of cloud began to mesh the sky.

'It's a long way back,' muttered Niall. 'Can they last this
long?'

'Some of them will,' said Finnglas, and set her mouth in
an obstinate line.

The ship came out of the mist on the first morning of
autumn, and the breeze lifted the vapour and streamed it
away like flags. Crisp blue sky was all about them, and in
front, the sparkle of spires, a city golden in the sun.

For a moment, Finnglas's hands fought the tiller. The sail
flapped and shuddered. She brought it taut again. The ship
swung in towards the land.

'Like a well-mewed falcon to the lure, or a dog to its
kennel,' Niall murmured. 'As if it were coming home.'

'Wherever it is, it's corn and hay,' said Finnglas. 'That's
all we've come for.'

Niall shaded his eyes.

'They're putting out to meet us.'

A fleet of fast ships sped from the harbour. Banks of oars
rowing against the wind. The ships were full of soldiers.
Grey helmets. Wolfskin cloaks.

'Turn the ship!' shouted Niall suddenly. 'Look at the wolf-
heads! Don't you see where we are? The ship has found her
home port!'

On every prow reared a figurehead like their own. Not
gold, but iron-grey.

'The helm won't turn!' Finnglas panted. 'There's nowhere

37

else for us to go.'

The leading ship was driving towards them. The grey wolf's head stared at them with bright eyes, ears pricked, tongue hanging red. A forest of spears sprouted. The ships closed. The soldiers sprang.

'A sword!' wailed Finnglas. 'If only I had my sword!'

'Thank God you haven't,' muttered Niall, retreating before the leaping tide of soldiers, his great hands swinging uselessly by his sides.

Pangur shot round the corner of the cabin. The soldiers were running after him, weapons raised. With one blow of those bright blades they could sever a white cat's head from his tail. Niall thundered behind them.

'Stop! Don't kill him!'

A grey-haired warrior turned, teeth bared.

'Who dares steal King Jarlath's flag-ship and deny us vengeance? What have you done with the captain?'

Pangur looked up, trembling, into a snarling face, a bristling beard. Niall's silence ended abruptly as the flat of the sword struck the side of his face, cutting his ear.

'You'll talk soon enough when the king gets you! Like a squealing rabbit. Move! Into the boat with the others!'

Pangur fled past him, following Finnglas and the bloodstained Niall, down into one of the galleys. Slaves rowed them ashore.

Behind them, the golden ship rode at its anchor in the harbour mouth. The gilded sail tumbled to the deck.

Grey streets. They marched in silence between the iron guard. Pale northern faces stared fearfully at them as they passed. A dazzle of golden gates clanging a hollow music as they swung shut behind them. Then cold stairs. A black dungeon. Water dripping from the walls. Silence.

'That's it,' said Niall, sitting down mournfully. 'We'll never get out of here alive.'

'I can explain to the king,' said Finnglas. 'I'll pay him for everything. I'm a king's daughter.'

'*What* can you explain?' mewed Pangur. 'That Arthmael gave us his ship as a present? That you want to fill it with his corn and pay him with his own gold? That you'll sail it away to Gwanegreth and he'll never see it again? Is *that* what you're going to tell him?'

He prowled the cell. High in the greasy walls an iron grating let in the wind. It was too high for him to spring up to the thick stone ledge.

'Lift me,' he ordered Niall.

The young monk's hand placed him on the ledge in the barred sunlight.

'What can you see?' asked Niall.

'A courtyard. A wall. A strip of sky. It's not what I can *see* that matters. It's where I can go.'

He squeezed through the bars and stood on the outside ledge. All at once he was back, pressing into the shadows, shaking with fear.

Grey legs went past the grating, stopped, came back. A face bent to the opening, grinning savagely.

'Wait till the Rhymester points his finger at you!'

He laughed long and low. A bell clanged. The grey legs went away.

Pangur was still trembling. 'It's all right for you. They'll keep you alive until you've talked. But they don't even know that I can!'

'Oh, hurry, Pangur!' called Finnglas from below. 'You've got to get us out! The lives of the horses hang on you!'

'I'm not Arthmael,' complained Pangur, squirming through the grille. 'Oh, why did he send us here?'

He looked nervously round. The soldier had gone. All round him rose the palace walls, stone-based, wooden-walled, with carved and gilded roofs. The courtyard was deserted.

But behind him a door crashed against a wall. Pangur leapt away from the grating. There was a cry from Finnglas. A harsher curse.

'Finnglas!' shouted Niall's voice.

Another oath. And then the door slammed shut. There was silence.

Pangur crept back and peered down. The cell was empty.

He padded across the courtyard feeling very alone. Would

the guards remember there had been a small white cat?

He put his nose cautiously round a corner. A second courtyard. Smells of cooking. A pile of rubbish in a corner that someone had tried to burn. Grey ashes, black charcoal. Pangur held his nose against the smell and rolled in the cinders, trying not to choke. He got to his feet again, a dusty grey cat. It was a thin disguise. But if he was to set Finnglas and Niall free, he must go back into the palace, under the eyes of the soldiers.

He crept on. Out at a side gate. And suddenly he was at the golden front of the palace. A flock of women in embroidered robes was going up a stairway flanked with wolf-cloaked guards like granite carvings. They were led by a pale, proud girl in a golden jacket.

He darted in among the coloured skirts. Up one step. There was whispering above him. Up two. Up three. The great door was swinging open before him. Like a small grey shadow he was slipping through.

The pale girl swung round. Her red skirt brushed over Pangur, raising a cloud of evil-smelling ash. She cried out in disgust.

And on the steps the helmets turned. Eyes widened. There was a shout of rage. Pangur, like a gust of wind, streaked into the palace. A spear slammed into the gilded oak of the door, scattering the shrieking women like a scythe through poppies. But he was inside.

There were cries in front of him. Servants running towards the noise. They pressed back to the walls in fear as the pack of shouting guards stormed in through the doors.

Pangur whisked through the running legs. Round a corner out of sight of the spears. Across a hall. There were more footsteps coming the other way. He skidded to a halt and leaped for a high window. The spears flashed into the room. The grey tide of soldiers went pouring past beneath him.

Pangur shook as the two parties collided round the next corner in a storm of cursing. There were swift barks of command. He heard the pursuing guards pound off into the distance. The slower steps came on.

Finnglas and Niall, heads lifted, faces set. Guarded by more warriors. Pangur shrank back into the angle of the window, a dusty shadow in the sunlight.

They had gone, and he was alone. The running guards, the frightened servants, the chattering noblewomen, had all drained away like storm water. In the room where he was, it was cool, dim, quiet. He wanted to stay.

But Finnglas and Niall were being dragged before the king. And on Gwanegreth of the Forgotten, the sack of corn was empty.

He jumped down and padded softly across the floor. It is not hard to find a king. You choose the widest doors, the lightest halls, the tallest windows. Even though your body screams for small, dark hiding-places.

Suddenly he heard Finnglas's high, commanding voice.

'We are not thieves! We have come to buy corn to save the horses.'

'*Buy*?' A voice like gravel grating on granite. 'You steal my own ship, and you talk to me of buying?'

Stealthily Pangur put his nose round the last corner. He was almost at the doorway. A glimpse through to a hall that gleamed with gold and stained glass windows. Grey ranks of wolf-cloaked guards. A rainbow cluster of women round the girl with the golden jacket. Then gold steps, gold dais, a golden throne. And Jarlath.

A gold-clad king, rising in anger from a golden throne. His cloak was crusted gold, richly wrought, heavily clasped with panels of figured gold. Gold slippers. Gold cap. But an iron-grey head. Grey beard. Eyes grey and wild as the sea in winter. And behind him, the shadow of himself, shrouded in grey, beneath a deep-set hood.

Pangur cringed back, more afraid of that tall shadow than of the king, as Finnglas's voice rose higher.

'I'll pay you anything you ask. For one shipload of corn. I've told you, the horses are *dying*!'

'What is that to me? In my stables there are a thousand corn-fed horses. Where is my captain?'

'I don't know. The ship was empty when we found it. Arthmael gave it to us to save the horses.'

'Who is Arthmael?'

Finnglas's voice rang through the hall.

'The dolphin. The great Dolphin with the scar down his side. The world's Fool. The Clown. He saved our lives.'

There was a rattle of breath. A voice colder than the king's, like hailstones upon the rocks. The grey shadow, taller than the king, reared above the throne.

'Comes the Dolphin now so close, whose breath
Our strongest spells would loose, whose dance is
death?'

'No,' said Niall, bewildered. 'You've got it all wrong. Arthmael gives life.'

'Now the Dolphin nears our net.
Jarlath's sea-wolves stalk him yet.
Do not seek his blood to save.
Speak now, where he stains the wave?'

'Finnglas, don't tell him!' cried Niall.

'As if I would!'

The grey hood swayed forward towards them both. Two red spots glowed out of its shadows. Even the king drew aside, pulling his gold cloak tighter as though to keep out a bitter wind. The voice grated like shingle dragged down by the undertow.

'If that false fisher once should dance
Within my reach, in Jarlath's realm,
I'll wake the wolf-pack from their trance
And his proud power overwhelm.'

In the shadow of the door, Pangur shuddered. Finnglas's
voice rose higher.

'I will not lead you to Arthmael. It is for corn we came.
If you will load the ship, my father will pay you royally.
But if you insult me, you will find a thousand warriors at
your gate! I am Finnglas, daughter of Kernac, princess of
the Summer Land.'

'A princess!' Sudden laughter swept the hall. The
noblewomen were shaking with merriment like flowers in
the wind. Even the guards were grinning at her. Only the
girl in the golden jacket was scowling.

The grey king howled.

'Have a care! I am Jarlath, King of the Wolves, the father
of princes. Look there at my daughter in her golden jacket.
Do you dare compare yourself to her? A princess? You,
Kernac's daughter! A wrinkled, dirty, brown, rotten
apple!'

'I tell you, my father is a king. If I still wore the sword
he gave me, you would not dare to speak to me so!'

'*What!*'

'You see? It is true. Only princesses speak like that,' Niall
said hastily. 'And I have skills to sell too. I am an artist.
The greatest in all Erin, so they tell me. Give me a
parchment and inks and I will illuminate you a Gospel page
richer than a prince's ransom. For a whole book of such
beauty you would pay a thousand ships of corn.'

'A scribe! A painter!' Again the gale of laughter shook the
crowd.

But Jarlath's voice rasped without laughter.

'Show me your hands . . . *painter*. Hold them out to my
daughter. There! Do you see how she shrinks back in
disgust? She cannot bear to see the blood creeping from
the cuts in your hands. An *artist's* hands? You dare thrust

43

those split, swollen, blistered joints under my nose and tell me that those fingers could hold a pen!'

Niall looked down sadly at his wounded hands.

'I *was* a painter, in a monastery, once. And Finnglas was a princess. She wears the six colours of the royal house. But you're right. That seems like another lifetime now . . . '

'What's that you say? A royal cloak? That scrap of filth and rags? You women! The cloak from her shoulders! Show it to me!'

Three noblewomen hurried forward. Before they could reach her, Finnglas's quick fingers unpinned the mantle. Her neck fell bare. The women started back.

'See! The royal gold about her throat!'

In trembling haste they laid the mantle at Jarlath's feet. It was stiff with salt, mud, ashes, matted into a hard grey shell, where once the soft new wool had been chequered with glowing dyes from the finest loom in the kingdom. Hands turned it over and explored the lining. Faint traces of colour lingered in the folds. Heads craned forward.

'It is true, King Jarlath! See here. There are threads of purple on yellow; scarlet and green crossed with blue; chequers of coal-black. It is the six-coloured plaid that only princes wear.'

For the first time Jarlath smiled. 'So! My wolf-ship has done well. She *is* a princess! And she comes to Senargad of the Golden Gates. Tell me . . . have you brothers . . . lady?'

'I had one. But he . . . died.'

Niall hung his head.

Jarlath came down the steps towards her. His long pale hand reached out.

'So much the better for me. Come higher . . . Queen Finnglas!'

Finnglas took a step back from him. The guards growled behind her.

'I am Kernac's *daughter*! A princess, not a queen.'

The grey eyes gleamed into hers.

'And I say you shall be *my* queen now.'

It must be a trick. She struggled to understand.

The king's head flicked round.

'How say you, Rhymester? Is it not fitting? She steals my crew and brings her monk instead. Shall I not take her for my own, since she comes so willingly? Make her pay for her theft with a wedding-ring? And with her hand, add Kernac's kingdom to my own? Is it not just?'

The grey shadow stepped before the king's gold throne, in the king's place. Close-hooded, stooped, hiding two burning eyes. Finnglas started to tremble.

The voice creaked like a frozen river, chilling the heart.

'Gold-decked they fared, as to a feast.
She comes as bride who brings her priest.'

'No!' cried Finnglas, horrified. 'No!'

11

Finnglas looked round wildly for help. The king's fingers closed round her wrist.

'And I say, *yes*. No, do not turn to my daughter. She will not plead for you. And I would spurn her if she did. She has brought me no joy, who cost her mother's life. Tomorrow you take that dead queen's place.'

Finnglas gave a great cry of protest.

'Never! I will not wed you! My father shall hear of this!'

The voice rasped. 'You dare say no to Jarlath of the Wolves? You do not know what I can do. Call your father? If I bid the Rhymester stretch out his finger, do you know what you shall become? A rabbit. Show her, Rhymester. Show her what will happen to her then.'

'No!' she tried to shut her eyes against that freezing voice.

But out of the sleeve the pale hand pointed. The light gleamed on curved black nails. Sharp as splinters, the ice-cold words pierced her brain.

> 'From the bitter hills and the cruel snow,
> Dealing death I make them go.
> Up from the dark, loosed from my thrall,
> *I raise the Wolf-Guard in this hall*!'

Finnglas's eyes opened suddenly wide in horror as the ranks of wolf-cloaked warriors leaped towards her. And in the act of springing they changed horribly. The wolf-cloaks streamed back into hairy flanks and tearing claws. The grey necks bristled with fury. Black gums bared, yellow teeth snarling, red tongues dripping saliva. A savage howl burst from a hundred throats of a raging pack of wolves. Two great paws slammed into her shoulders and she felt their hot breath on her face.

Pangur screamed as Finnglas's white, terrified face disappeared beneath the leaping muzzles, the snapping fangs. But the sound was lost in the shrieks of Jarlath's women.

'Enough! Get back! The woman cowers.
The breath of Jarlath's pack teach her my powers.'

The burning eyes retreated within their shroud. The wolves cringed to the floor and backed away. A hundred pairs of flattened ears, a hundred open jaws, still growling threateningly, ringed the prostrate form of Finnglas. Niall helped her to her feet. They were both shaking with fear.

Jarlath laughed at them then, like icicles breaking from the eaves.

'You see, *Princess*. A rabbit does not send for warriors. It has no time. You will wed me tomorrow.'

'No!' Finnglas wept. 'No! You cannot do this! I am a free woman of the Summer Land. No one can wed me where I do not choose. Not even the king, my father!'

'You came of your own free will. You brought your priest. The laws of your land do not run in Jarlath's kingdom.'

'You know why I came! To but corn for the horses. Only for that and nothing else!'

For the last time the freezing voice creaked from the hood.

> 'Then take the dolphin's friend to wife,
> And let her sail the dark whale's way.
> She lures him to the last of life.
> The Sea-Wolves rise and end his day.'

'No! *No*! I will never betray Arthmael! I will not lead you to him.'

'Then the horses will die.'

'No! You cannot make her!' Niall protested.

The wolves snarled.

Pangur crouched shuddering in the doorway, too horrified to move. Slowly the nearest wolf lifted its muzzle. Sniffed the air curiously. Turned. And the red eyes saw Pangur.

With a howl of fury, the whole pack was on its feet. Pangur shrieked and fled. Out of the great doors, leaving a trail of ashen prints across the hall. And now the chase began, deadlier than ever, with the slavering muzzles questing for his scent. Above the courtyard he checked in terror. The steps were lined with wolves now. Then he was flying between their startled jaws, like a blown cinder on the wind. Across the yard, springing for a window above the snarling, snapping fangs. Another ledge, over a gargoyle. Climbing, scrabbling. A baffled baying growing fainter behind him. Up the sloping thatch, leaping for another roof, over the ridge and on and up, to the greatest roof of all. Higher and higher, beyond pursuit . . .

And face to face with another wolf.

Pangur nearly fell backwards off the roof. He drew a gasping breath.

Gold. Only a carved and gilded wolf-head, crowning Jarlath's great hall. Pangur slipped down a little, trembling with relief, and dug his claws into the new golden thatch.

He listened. The distant hubbub was dying. He tried to quiet his shivering. He raised his head and looked about him. And his tail stiffened in the wind. Below was the grey harbour, and Jarlath's ship riding empty at its mouth. But over the roofs of the city, beyond the walls, the hills stood pregnant with corn. And a line of wagons, stacked with living gold, was rolling down towards the town. Pangur watched them come nearer, laden high as houses with piled sheaves. Watched the gates swing open and the city square receive them. Watched the great doors of Jarlath's barns gape blackly and the slaves begin to fork the harvest in. King Jarlath's corn, for King Jarlath's city and King Jarlath's horses. If only Finnglas could see this!

And even as he thought it, Finnglas's voice rose desperately beneath him.

'No!'

'Tomorrow!'

'No! No!'

Niall's shout. 'Let her go!'

A sharp cry. A fierce burst of snarling. Jarlath's voice again, grinding like shingle in a storm.

'Quick! Seize them both! Have a care of that monk! So. Now take them both away and keep them close. Prepare her for tomorrow.'

'*Miaow*!' wailed Pangur in despair, above the clatter of retreating footsteps and Finnglas's frantic cries.

There was a sudden hush below. The footsteps halted. Pangur shrank back. Then the wolves howled, more furiously than ever. But they could not smell him, perched out of sight on the eaves above the window. The din surged past and the hall fell silent. At last, from a distant corner of the palace, Niall's voice rose like a roll of thunder in a psalm.

> *'Hear my prayer, O Lord; let my cry come to thee!*
> *Do not hide they face from me in the day of my*
> *distress!'*

The sound of a blow, and an angry snarl. The psalm broke off short. But Pangur managed a shaky smile. He had a fine, carrying voice, had Niall. He was a difficult man to hide. One tower stood alone in the northwest corner of the palace. The second window from the top.

And Finnglas?

Pangur crouched unseen beneath the gargoyle and waited, while the sun dropped down the sky.

12

At sunset the psalm rose for the second time.

'Oh, give thanks to the Lord, for he is good.
For his steadfast love endures for ever.'

Pangur picked his way over the steep roofs towards the sound of Niall's voice. Before he got there, the chant ended suddenly with an oath that Drusticc would have given a monk penance for. Then there was silence.

Pangur stopped and looked about him in the autumn twilight. The thatch was beaded with damp and the white stubble fields beyond the city were turning grey. Already the harbour was disappearing in the mist. Pangur shivered. But picking up his paws delicately he went on. In the far northwest corner of the patchworked courtyard stood the high, square wooden tower, with a pointed roof.

He stood, wobbling slightly, on the end of the last roof ridge, looked across, and caught his breath sharply. Through the window of the tower opposite he could see Niall, squatting on the floor. Before him two great wolves were sprawled, their heads on their paws, watching the door with their backs to the window.

Niall's face leapt into life as he saw Pangur, and at once fell calm. Slowly, he lifted his hand to scratch his ear. For a brief moment his finger pointed to the ceiling above him. Pangur nodded.

It was a long leap to the sill of the window from the roof ridge. He almost missed, and hung clinging by his front claws. Niall watched helplessly. Pangur hoisted himself to safety and climbed on, up to the highest window of all. He looked over his shoulder at the swirling mist. Was there no one to help him? If only Arthmael was here. If he called now, would the great dolphin hear him across the sea and come? But no, he must not come where the Rhymester ruled.

But Finnglas had already seen him on the window-ledge and came running across to lift him in.

'Ssh!' he warned, and purred violently as he rubbed himself against her familiar shoulder.

'Oh, Pangur Bán! Thank goodness you've come!' She hugged him tightly. 'You've got to help me. You're all I've got. I must get out of here tonight. It's not just me. The horses . . . Arthmael . . . If I don't . . .'

'I know. I heard it all.' He wriggled down to the floor. 'But what can I do? I'm only a very small cat.'

'All I need is a rope. If you could climb up the tower with the end in your mouth . . .'

'But I haven't *got* a rope.'

'It's a port, isn't it? There are ships. Of course there'll be rope!'

'And after you've climbed down this rope, what about Niall? There are wolves guarding the room below.'

'I don't know. Perhaps if we made a commotion in the yard . . . They might come running to see what had happened, and we might set him free.'

'And if we don't?'

'Oh, how do I know? I can't think of everything. Oh, hurry up, Pangur! I've got to get out before morning!'

Pangur looked nervously over the edge of the window sill.

'It's all very well to say, hurry up. Hurrying *up* is easy. It's hurrying *down* that's the problem when you've got four feet.'

'You can do it. You climbed the mast of Jarlath's ship.'

'Don't rush me.'

His paws were slithering on the greasy angles of wet wood. Claws digging for a hold, his weight pulling at their roots. The world facing him upside-down.

Then a shout from below. A human shout. Fear catching him off balance. A rock slammed into his shoulder, pinning him against the wall, and then cruelly released him. With a howl of pain and panic he went hurtling out into an immense grey, tumbling, stone-paved space.

He struck the ground, and the breath spat from his body like pulp from a squashed fruit. He lay still, like a torn white rag in the gloom of the courtyard. Then there were feet running towards him. The ground beneath him shook. He tried to rise, and screamed with the pain in his shoulder. Hands seized him tightly, squeezing his agonized ribs. With a last convulsive twitch, like a sick trout, he slithered between the grasping fingers and was away across the courtyard. Pain at every step. Limping on bruised paws. Wanting to howl, but the tearing breath in his lungs leaving him no voice. Round the corner into the shadows. Where were the wolves? Across an open space. The golden gate was shut now. Under it . . .

And the howling broke out behind him. The gates flew open and the baying pack were at his heels. The street was too empty to hide.

As he raced down the hill it began to rain. A few, fat, heavy drops and then a deluge as the drought of summer ended. Now water was chasing him faster than the running wolves. Sluicing down the gutterless streets in a slimy tide. Garbage floating. Cabbage leaves catching his legs. Sticks, autumn leaves. His feet were slithering. He was falling, splashing, swimming. A piece of wood struck him from behind and wedged itself under his knees. He leaned his weight on it and eased himself back till he could lay his saturated head down at last. He ceased to struggle and let the raft spin him away into the darkness towards the sea. Behind him, the baying grew more distant, less certain. Darkness came from inside his head, blacker than the growing night.

When he opened his eyes, it was with the sudden shock of lying still. As he tried to move he cried out once and then was fearfully silent. The last of the light glimmered at the sea's edge. He was lying in a dirty puddle on the wooden staithe.

Gritting his teeth against the pain, he limped on over the slippery logs. The rain had flattened the sea, hissing like iron in the blacksmith's forge. Out in the middle of the harbour a tall grey shape was moored. The shadow of the golden ship. A fleet of fishing boats was tied along the staithe. Even if he escaped with his life, it was past his imagining how he could carry a rope back to the palace now. And the howls were coming nearer.

He passed an empty boat. Then two more. Hurrying. Then three. Running now, in spite of the pain. Four. Five. Six. And in the seventh, a heap of wet canvas, a tangle of fishing lines, and a coil of almost new rope.

Pangur looked over his shoulder. And the tide of wolves, like a nightmare, swept round the corner.

His body shrank from the leap. In spite of himself he could not stop the shout of pain as he landed with the jarring agony of wood on cracked bone. He dived for the dark centre of the coil of rope.

The canvas erupted.

'Got you! What are you doing in my boat?' a voice cried from beneath it.

This time hands gripped his body in a grasp so sure that no cat, not even a squirming fish, could hope to escape.

13

Pangur's heart beat against his bruised ribs like a frantic robin trapped inside a house. Again and again he struggled as the wolves bayed nearer, fear stronger than the pain. But it was no use. These hands knew their work. He went suddenly limp.

'That's better,' said the voice. 'Keep your claws to yourself.'

He felt himself set down on a warm knee. But the hands did not relax. Cautiously he opened an eye.

The heap of wet canvas had sat up and opened, revealing a boy with tousled ginger hair.

'What were you doing?' he said. 'Have you come to steal my fish?'

Pangur looked swiftly back. The wolves were running across the staithe, questing, howling, hunting. He made up his mind.

'No. Stealing your rope. To save a princess,' he said.

The boat rocked sharply and the hands let go. Pangur dived through the crook of the boy's arm into the dark folds of canvas.

Above the boat there was a heavy panting through the rain. Many wolves sniffing, growling.

'Who's that down there?' barked one of them suddenly.

There was a splash as the boy hastily dropped a fishing line over the side.

'Young Erc, that was Big Erc's son,' he called up. 'Fishing for my supper.'

'Have you seen a cat go past? A dirty white cat?'

'Not a rat, or a sprat,' said Erc.

'Don't be funny with me!'

'No cat has passed my boat.'

54

There was a low growl from many throats. Vile snuffling, scouring the rain-washed planks, insistent, suspicious. Slowly, very slowly, they moved away.

Pangur crept out of hiding. Erc looked down at him thoughtfully.

'Stealing my rope, I thought you said.'

'Yes.'

'To save a princess.'

'That's right.'

'And the wolves are after you.'

Pangur nodded.

'Then King Jarlath must have got her.'

'In a tower as high as the tree-tops. And he's going to marry her against her will tomorrow. Unless I can get her out.'

'He would. That's the sort of king he is. My father was lost at sea in a storm this summer. And my mother couldn't pay the king's tax to build his golden palace. So he told her he would sell me as a slave, and sent his wolves to fetch me. But I was away at the fishing in my father's boat. I would have paid him! But he wouldn't wait. King Jarlath never waits. When I got home, he had sold my mother to the slavers for more gold, and the slave-ship had sailed away. I don't even know where they have taken her.'

Erc was silent. Pangur rubbed his head against the boy's chest.

Erc swallowed, and went on more brightly, 'So. You want a rope to rescue this princess?'

'Yes.' Pangur took a deep breath. 'Only . . . Well . . . I've hurt myself. They threw stones at me, and I fell off the tower. I can't walk very well. If you could carry me back to the palace . . . and the rope, of course.'

'Oh! Anything else?'

'Well, the gates are shut, and the wolves are guarding them now. If you could help me break into the palace . . . '

'Go on!'

'And get the princess out.'

'And then?'

'Well, yes. You see, it's not just the princess. There's a monk as well. In a room with two wolves. If you could help me rescue him . . . '

'Is that *all*?'

'N-no. As a matter of fact, we came here to buy corn. Enough to save a hundred starving horses. I don't think Finnglas will leave without it.'

Erc was speechless. Pangur hesitated.

'And . . . I hardly like to mention it. But we'll need a boat. To get away. We came in King Jarlath's.'

There was a long silence.

'I see. And are you *sure* there's nothing else?'

'I don't think so. But if I remember, I'll let you know.' He held his breath.

Erc stood up and pulled the tarpaulin closer about him.

'Right. Then if we're going to get through that lot tonight, we'd better get started.'

He put the coil of strong rope round his shoulder, and tucked Pangur carefully under the other arm. The tarpaulin hid them both. He climbed out of the boat and climbed up the hill through the darkness and the rain to Jarlath's stronghold.

14

They avoided the golden gate and skirted the wall. The rain blew raggedly over the jagged spikes that crested it. Erc halted, and lifted his head.

The moon was hidden deep behind rushing clouds. But every now and then the wind tore them apart, and the night was silvered for a moment. In one such gleam a steep-pitched roof towered above their heads, with a carved gable-end. In the blink of an eye, Erc had cast his rope.

Twice the wet rope came slithering down the roof into his hands. But at the third break in the clouds he hitched the gable-prow securely. He picked up Pangur.

'You'll have to come with me to show me where the princess is.'

A swaying rope, the agony of his ribs, clutching at Erc, a climbing roof, a gentle slide down, the last painful thud. Listening for wolves.

Erc turned, lifting the heavy latch behind him and opened the great door a little way. The rich smell of new-sheaved corn sweetened the air.

'The corn!' squeaked Pangur. 'It's the barn with all the corn.'

'Is it?' whispered Erc. 'Well, it's your way out. That's more important. And I suppose *that's* where he's got your princess.'

The tower opposite loomed blackly against the clouds, impossibly high. At its foot, the courtyard was a dark, dangerous lake. Lights gleamed from the windows of the hall revealing panels of driving rain. Erc swished quickly across to the darkest corner and began to climb by ledges and carvings.

He reached the great roof. The highest windows of the

tower were now above them, separated from them by a river of drumming rain.

'The roof's too high to catch the rope,' muttered Erc.

'Last time, I jumped,' Pangur whispered back. 'But that was before they hurt my shoulder. And I almost missed then.'

There was a tiny glow in the window.

'Finnglas?' called Pangur softly.

No one answered. He dared not call louder.

'I could throw you across,' said Erc gently. 'If you wanted me to.'

Pangur swallowed.

'It seems a pity to come all this way for nothing.'

Very gently, Erc knotted the rope about the cat's body. His knuckles rubbed behind the white ears.

'Good luck, little cat.'

And he tossed him out into the darkness.

Pangur's ribs seemed to scream aloud as his paws hit the first window-ledge and hung there braced. He began to climb. As the cracked bones opened and the torn muscles took the weight of his body, he sent his mind away into other worlds. To Arthmael leaping through the sunlit spray. To a winter night in a convent by the sea, and himself warm and well-fed on Niall's lap. To Finnglas's dead brother, Martin . . . He cried out in anguish.

But it was only his back legs slipping in the wet, leaving his whole weight hanging from one damaged shoulder. He dug his claws in and went on.

The highest window-sill. A room lit by one candle. A last jarring leap down on to the floor.

'Who's that?'

But the silhouette leaping from the bed was not Finnglas's. The flowing skirt, the hanging sleeves, two braided plaits glinting with strands of gold. A stranger.

With a muffled cry, Pangur leaped back to the sill. But he was not quick enough. He tried not to scream as the hands swept him up and hugged him.

'Finnglas! It *is* you!'

'Of course it's me! They took my cloak away from me,

and my tunic and boots. They washed me and dressed me like one of their noblewomen. Embroidered skirts. Jewelled plaits. *Slippers*! Have you brought the rope?'

And she was swarming over the sill. He heard the gasp as she landed. She had found Erc at the foot of the tower.

They had left him behind. He was a small white flag hanging from the window.

'Jump!' hissed Erc. 'The princess will catch you in her skirt.'

Was that a growl from the room below? He let himself fall.

'The barn!' Erc pushed Finnglas forward.

'But we have to get Niall out.'

'Do as I tell you. Quick!'

'How dare you give orders to me!' she stormed in a whisper. 'I'm a princess!'

'The *barn* . . . your highness! And out through the roof. It's a princess and a cat they're looking for. Not a nobody with ginger hair.'

'It's a matter of honour!'

'It's a matter of commonsense.'

They glared at each other in the darkness.

A second growl rumbled from the tower.

'Finnglas,' murmured Pangur in her ear. 'There's corn in that barn.'

'Corn? *Where*?'

And she was off, running through the rain, shaking Pangur cruelly.

They slipped through the half-open door. The sweet scent met them. Finnglas thrust her hands into the rustling darkness.

'Corn! Smell it! Feel it, Pangur! It's all we want!'

A great yowl split the night outside. 'MIAOW!'

'It's Erc!' gasped Pangur. 'What is he doing?'

From the yard there was a moment's silence, and then pandemonium. Wolves barking, feet running, doors flying open.

'The cat! The cat!'

Pangur pushed Finnglas up the sloping stack of sheaves.

59

They scrambled to the top and lay flat beneath the rafters.

Lights sprang up in windows, burst out of doors, zigzagged like flies across the streaming darkness. An old slave tottered out, his lantern wavering uncertainly. Erc seized it from him, dashed into the tower, and pounded up the stairs. Two wolves sprang through the doorway above him, teeth bared in a snarl.

'The princess! She's escaped!' Erc shouted to them. 'There's a rope from her window!'

The wolves whirled round and bounded over Niall, back to the window. Erc grabbed the monk by the hand and dragged him downstairs. He dropped the lantern. They were running now through the shouting mêlée. Brushing past wolves snapping in blind rage. In through the barn door. Erc pulled it quietly shut.

In panting haste they started to climb. Fresh sheaves cascaded beneath them, covering their scent.

'Niall?' Finnglas's whisper was sharp with doubt.

A hairy knee and a wet brown robe descended on Pangur. Hands tore at the thatch above. But before the moon could break through, the great door crashed open.

'Warriors can't *smell*!' moaned Pangur.

They threw themselves flat.

Again that furious snuffling. Paws scrabbling through the straw. Tongues panting.

Their leader barked once.

Slaves came hastening with pitchforks. Jabbing, thrusting. Rain dripped from Niall's head rustling into the grain. The sounds below were more vicious.

'If they were there, they're either skewered or suffocated.'

The door swung shut. The snarling moved further off.

In a few more moments Niall had made a hole into the night. He and Pangur squeezed through and dropped into squelching mud below the wall. As they slid down the thatch, Pangur heard Finnglas's voice rise behind him.

'But the corn! There must be sacks! We've got to take the corn!'

Next moment she came rolling down the roof in a tumble of flying skirts. Niall caught her as she fell.

'I'm sorry about that, your highness,' said Erc, jumping down beside her. 'But there's no time to waste.'

'How dare you! I'm going back! I've got to get the corn! Don't you understand? I'd rather die myself than go back without it. I can't stand by and watch those horses starve.'

Erc seized her by the arm and started to run. 'We're wasting time. The corn is already on board.'

15

Niall and Pangur stared after him in astonishment. But already he and Finnglas were disappearing down the steep, grass-grown hill. In a few moments they would be left behind, with the slavering wolves, and the grey king who sold his people for gold, and the pointing Rhymester. Desperately they ran after him, slipping and sliding on the grass.

Finnglas stopped suddenly. The others nearly fell over her.

'I've got to go back!' she whispered. 'The horses! Jarlath said he had a thousand horses. She might be . . .'

There was a tense silence.

'Finnglas. Melisant is dead,' Pangur said softly. 'Think of the living.'

They heard Finnglas draw her breath in a long, shaking sob. Then she started to run again, down the hill.

Fog thickened wetly about them. There was mud underfoot, cold between their toes. Then stones, and seaweed, pools of water. They were on a beach.

Erc pushed them behind a huge boulder.

'Stay here. Don't move. I'll be as quick as I can.' And he was gone.

Hours seemed to pass. The rain stopped. There was only the sound of the sucking tide. The thick darkness of the fog turned to ashen grey, and then to white, and the sky overhead began to change to the colour of the first bluebells. At any moment the morning sun would burst through.

Then, from the hidden sea, came the creak of oars.

Niall gripped Finnglas's arm. Pangur felt his fur stiffen. Not a sound came from the approaching boat but the muffled splash of steady rowing.

The boat bumped gently against the stones.

'Your highness? . . . Pangur Bán? . . . Niall?'

In a burst of joy they tumbled out to meet him. Pangur recognized the little brown boat. They scrambled on board.

Erc rowed the boat out into mid-stream. The water lay like satin all around them, the fog a lime-washed wall roofed with blue sky. Erc look up at the mast-head.

'It's going to be a fine day.'

Presently he stopped rowing and listened. Very gently he lifted the oars on board and set them down without a sound. He knelt in the bows, peering ahead. His hands softly paddled the water. The boat crept slowly forward.

Suddenly he seemed to dive over the side, leaving only his legs behind. There was a glint of a small blade in his hand. And Pangur saw, climbing out of the water, a huge cable stretching up higher than the fishing boat's mast. A moment later the rope fell slack and out of the fog a towering grey wall seemed to glide towards them. Erc paddled furiously and the terrified passengers saw the sides of a great ship loom over them. Its deck was shrouded in mist. No sound came from it. And now they were at the bows, and another hawser. Silently Erc sawed at it, while the others listened, hearts straining, minds questioning, on the edge of panic.

Then the strands snapped and Erc was passing the dripping rope to Niall, frantically signalling to him to make it fast. As the painter's salt-sore fingers laboured at the unwieldy thickness, Erc took an oar and began to pole silently through the silk-smooth water. There was the very slightest check, and the rope tautened. The great ship began to follow them, like a cow to milking.

Erc motioned to Finnglas for the other oar and settled himself to row. Smoothly, steadily, almost soundlessly, and the air grew brighter and the sea began to shine. Finnglas was smiling, as if she knew. Niall was staring curiously up at their huge grey prisoner. Next moment the sun broke through the mist, swirling it away, and before their eyes the grey ship turned to gold. Golden shrouds, gilded cabin, the gold-encrusted wolf-head staring over them.

'The ship of gold!' Finnglas and Niall cried together.

And with their shout the ship sprang into life.

Two of Jarlath's grey-helmeted soldiers came running on to the deck, shouting in alarm.

'They're only men!' gasped Pangur in relief. 'Not wolves.'

Next moment a spear came whistling through the air. Niall threw his huge weight across the boat. It heeled violently till the gunwale hit the water. The spear went streaking past Erc's right ear and disappeared beneath the waves.

'You spoke too soon,' said Niall grimly as the little boat righted itself. '*Look out!*'

The next spear struck the mast.

Erc rowed furiously, stretching out the length of gleaming water between the two boats with the hawser tight. The men drew their swords. Pangur backed into the bows, waiting terrified for the first one to spring.

But they cupped their hands to their mouths and yelled. A ringing, desolate call that echoed dismally back to them from the mist.

Finnglas leaped to her feet, sudden hope brightening her face.

'They don't know how to sail the ship! There are only two of them. Look, they're afraid of us!'

But Erc's back bent faster and faster to his task, rowing for all he was worth out to sea. His face was streaming with sweat. The tops of the hills were swimming out of the mist. They were still too close to the shore. The soldiers bellowed louder to the waking town. And the wind began to rise, breaking the mist into tatters. The waves were sparkling, slapping the sides, lifting, breaking into spray. And out of the speedwell blue of the new morning, Jarlath's city broke into view with the sunlight dazzling on its golden spires.

As the two ships foamed towards the harbour mouth, an answering howl came thinly through the cold, clear air.

Erc's exhausted shoulders let the oars drop with a clatter into the boat.

'The sail!' he panted. 'We've got a wind at last! Hoist the sail!'

In a moment, with hands now practised, Niall and Finnglas were running the patched red sail up the mast. But even as it climbed, Niall shouted over his shoulder,

'It's no use! We sailed into harbour yesterday. We'll never sail out against the wind!'

'Landlubber!' Erc cried joyfully. 'Can't you feel it on your face? The year has turned! The wind is blowing from the north!'

The breeze filled the red sail cheerfully. They set it on a broad reach and the two ships, locked together, strained for the harbour mouth. As they swept through the rocks the great tumbling ocean lay before them. Finnglas and Niall sent up a welcoming cheer, and the two sentries yelled in fear.

But Erc looked over his shoulder, stiffened and caught his breath. The mist had vanished. And out of the dark blue shadows beyond the staithe came a pack of sharp-prowed galleys. Sleek, swift, powered by both yellow sail and flashing oars, with countless warrior wolves baying in the bows.

'So Jarlath has loosed his Sea-Wolves,' said Erc shuddering. 'Now may Lok the Lucky have mercy on the hunted!'

16

'They're closing,' said Niall, licking his dry lips.

Erc looked up at the great ship yawing in their wake.

'She'll take the wind from our sails if she thrashes about like that,' he muttered. 'It's time we got on board and sailed her.'

'Look!' cried Finnglas suddenly. 'The soldiers! They're cutting the rope!'

'And a good thing too!' wailed Pangur. 'Help them! Cut it loose! We might still escape!'

Finnglas stamped her foot. 'But didn't you hear what Erc said? That ship is full of corn. Can't you smell it? If we lose it, the horses will die.'

'But they'll capture *us*. *We'll* die.'

'Give me your knife,' said Niall to Erc. 'And lower the sail. Hurry.'

'No, Niall . . . !' Finnglas started to protest. 'You're not a fighting man. Let me.!'

Erc stared at him questioning, but the sail was already tumbling, and a rocking silence filled the boat as the wind left it.

'Be quick,' said Erc. 'They're gaining fast.'

As the hawser slackened and the tall bows swam towards them, Niall began to climb. The small silver knife was gripped in his teeth. Two iron swords stopped hacking at the rope and waited, raised.

His head neared the gunwale, beneath the wolf-head. The first warrior lunged, slashing at the monk's wrist. Niall stabbed wildly upwards, swinging one-handed from the rope. Pangur mewed desperately.

Without warning, the ship of gold lurched over on its side as if a sudden squall had hit it. The knife went spinning out of Niall's hand as he clutched frantically at the rope. There was a howl of terror above his head as the soldier was catapulted into the air, somersaulting over and over till he struck the waves. Slowly his sword sank beneath him, down through the depths. The ship righted itself. The fishing boat still bobbed unharmed.

'What made it do *that*?' gasped Finnglas.

As the frayed rope steadied, Niall was over the bows. The second sentry backed against the cabin, sword grasped. Niall was rocking on the balls of his feet, arms bared to the elbow, hands widespread, like a wrestler. Finnglas was already gripping the rope.

With a roar, the second warrior charged, and as he sprang the ship heeled violently the other way. The soldier, caught off balance, hurtled against the mast, knocking the breath from his body. He crashed to the deck, and his sword skidded away into the stern.

In a flash, Finnglas was up the rope, embroidered skirts hitched high round her waist, to stand beside Niall. Erc and Pangur came tumbling over the rail. The soldier reached for his dagger.

The newcomers drew their breath sharply. From here they could see the line of approaching galleys. The open jaws of the wolf-prows, the driving blades of the oars, the bowed backs of the slaves. The red-rimmed eyes of Jarlath's wolves.

In silent haste they sent the gold sail climbing, the blazoned wolf-head spreading, catching the wind. Like a goaded horse the ship lunged and sprang away.

Finnglas stared up at the sail. 'I don't understand it. The wind is doing strange things today . . . if it *is* the wind.'

'We need the tiller,' said Erc.

The four of them spread themselves in a line. They began to advance upon the stern.

'Get back,' growled the soldier.

His eyes flicked from one face to another. They flashed. His cloak streamed behind him as he leaped for Niall's throat.

But Pangur Bán leapt faster. Hurling himself through the air on to the warrior's helmet. Blinding his eyes with white fur. Clinging, scratching, biting. The soldier whirled round cursing, shook, twisted, flung his arms upwards and hurled Pangur from him. With a yowl, the cat was flying helplessly over the rail, falling, seeing the ocean beneath him.

The sun was blotted out. A rushing darkness swallowed him. He felt himself swept sideways, as if in a gale. Jaws snapped shut, but not on flesh, imprisoning him. There was a crash, as the sea exploded beyond the jaws. Water rushed past him. A deep green darkness outside, a fearful safety within. Then light above. The jaws opened on a dazzling sky and tossed him high into the air again.

Finnglas snatched him from the sky as he dropped for the second time. They both stared down.

Between the glittering waves rose a long, shining beak, a bottle nose, lifting, leaping to the height of the deck and falling back, laughing at them.

'Arthmael!' they cried together.

Fear surged through Pangur.

'Arthmael! They mean to kill you! The Sea-Wolves are coming!'

The warrior was hanging from the rail, scrabbling frantically for a hold. He fell back into the water with a splash. The dolphin whisked round to the stern and jumped out of the water. Erc reached down a hand. The dolphin's head rose and touched it lovingly.

'Lok the Lucky!' Erc whispered, awestruck.

The wind sprang stronger in the sail.

'He's Arthmael,' said Pangur.

They stared at each other.

'You know him too?' said Erc. 'Even where you come from?'

The dolphin leaped from the sea and danced in front of their flying bows. His long side was furrowed with scars. He winked at them.

'Know him?' said Finnglas incredulously. '*Know* him? He saved our lives.'

'And the Rhymester's going to kill him!'

With Erc's hand on the tiller, the ship flew from the wolves like a hind from the hounds. But she was wide-bellied, built for cargo not for speed. Erc's fishing boat bumped forlornly against her side. The sharp-prowed galleys strained after them, nosing ever closer across the gap. The sea between them was cold under the wind, narrowing, narrowing. The leading wolf bayed.

'The dolphin! The dancing dolphin! After him!'

Arthmael circled the ship madly, glancing back over his shoulder.

'We'll never make it,' shouted Niall. 'They're faster than we are. Save yourself, Arthmael!'

Erc glanced despairingly down.

'Cut the rope,' he ordered.

The others stared at him.

'But it's your boat. Your father's boat.'

'How will you get home? How will you live?'

Erc looked back. The wolves, sensing victory, were creeping up into the bows. Their mouths opened in dripping rows of teeth. Red eyes measured the distance to spring.

'I have no home. Cast off. Now!'

The severed rope went flying through the air. Slowly the two ships parted. The small brown boat drifted astern, seeming to float backwards into the advancing wolf-pack. The leading prow crashed into it and spent it spinning through the fleet, with the sound of splintering wood.

'We will pay you for it,' cried Finnglas.

Erc bit his lip and turned his face away.

'*Finnglas*!' said Pangur reproachfully.

'I'm sorry. Oh, Erc, I'm sorry!' said Finnglas.

With a new gift of speed the ship went foaming forward, with Arthmael racing through the green depths in front of her surging bows. But the wind that swept her along swept the galleys even faster. Still they came on. Three wavelengths separated them. The leading wolf gathered his shoulders to jump. Finnglas rushed to the bows.

'Arthmael! We can't lose now! Help us!'

'No, Arthmael! Save yourself!'

A spear struck the wave. The dolphin leaped out of the

sea and fell back in a fountain of spray, drenching her.

'What do you want me to do? Sing to them?'

'Arthmael! *Please*!'

He rolled over on to his back.

'You've hurt my feelings. Don't you *like* my singing?'

The ship raced past him. The wolves bayed in triumph. Finnglas ran to the stern.

'Don't be a fool, Arthmael! There isn't time!'

'There isn't time for anything else.'

He lifted his face to the sky and opened his blowhole. A comical whistle rose, more piercing than the wind. Higher and higher it soared, till it was lost beyond the reach of human hearing. Then Arthmael dived.

The wolves sprang, like a sea-wave bursting a dyke. Niall hurled a water-cask at the leader. It hung, toppling, on the gunwale, eyes red with fury. But the rail bristled with leaping wolves. The galleys swept round them, taking their wind. Oars crashed against the side. There were red tongues and yellow fangs on every side.

'Arthmael! Save us!' screamed Finnglas.

'Look!' shouted Erc.

From the four corners of the compass, huge, black, gleaming bodies were hurtling through the sea, churning the waves before them, building them up into an avalanche of foam. In the galleys the baying turned to howls of terror. The slaves yelled out in fright. Oars clashed as the close-packed ships fought to turn. The ring of towering breakers raced nearer. Wolves were dropping from the rail, claws tearing the wood. Slaves dived overboard, fighting to escape.

The green wall of water erupted in a hundred volcanoes. A ring of grinning heads rose from its crest. A hundred hump-backed whales bore down on them. Their broad, sleek skulls reared high above the galleys and hurtled down, smashing them into splinters. They dived beneath, tossing the broken ships up on their backs like toys. Their fluked tails rose behind them and lashed sideways, crumpling the masts, capsizing the hulls, spinning the wreckage round in whirlpools. The sea foamed and the air was rent with crashes, howls, screams.

The wind dropped. The sounds died into gurgles and splashing. All around was a ring of implacably smiling whales. Bits of broken wood began to float past, and drowning wolves and men.

17

'Horrible,' shuddered Niall. 'This was work for the Sea-Witch.'

Finnglas was listening to the cries from the water. Her face was white but determined.

'We have to turn back and pick them up,' she said.

'Are you mad?' cried Niall. 'Those wolves would murder us! Or take us back to the Rhymester, which would be worse.'

'I can't help it. Listen! They're drowning! I can't bear it. Not after I let Melisant . . . Erc, turn the ship!'

'Don't be a fool, Finnglas!' wailed Pangur.

'That's not the way your father taught you to wage war,' protested Niall.

Arthmael's face rose level with hers. It was silvered with tears.

'Don't listen to them, Finnglas. Be a fool!'

'I am no man's prisoner, not even my father's,' cried Finnglas. 'Turn the ship round.'

But the ship would not swing into the breeze. All they could do was cast down ropes and nets and wait for the survivors to struggle to them. For many it was too great an effort. The draggled remnants were hauled on board. The slaves gasped their gratitude. The huddled wolves, their wet coats plastered to their bodies, growled low in their throats and glared at their rescuers. But their red eyes kept slipping sideways to where the whales swam in a watchful circle, grinning still.

Arthmael vaulted over the bows, brushing the figurehead.

'Brother Wolf, I need every ounce of your speed now. To Gwanegreth!'

'The horses!' cried Finnglas. 'I forgot the horses! Oh, Erc!

72

Is the corn really on board?'

With a laugh, Erc seized her hand and ran with her aft. He drew the cover from the hatch and she leaned over. The warm golden smell of sun-ripe grain rose up to them.

'All yesterday I sat on the staithe and watched them load her. Straight from the fields to the ship.'

Niall peered down into the hold and scratched his head. 'The old devil! So Jarlath kept his promise, after all.'

'Oh, yes! He kept his promise,' said Finnglas bitterly. 'I knew he would. Don't you see? The price was Arthmael's blood. To save the horses, I had to betray Arthmael. If I had refused, the horses would have died. I could not save them both.'

A bubble of laughter rose from the stern.

'What Finnglas could not do, Arthmael can! Behold, the horses and I are both alive. Now, go, and be thankful!'

The last spit of land shot out to meet them. They left the slaves on the headland and the wolves on an island beyond. The whales waved their fluked tails in farewell and dived away.

And now it was as if the ship felt their need. The wind from the north had the cutting edge of autumn. The great sail strained before it, and flying spray-salt crusted the gilded mast. Finnglas shivered before it in her strange bridal clothing. The ship fled across the ocean under a clear blue sky, like a wild goose to its wintering, with Arthmael diving through the waves before their bows.

At last the bare bluffs of Gwanegreth showed above the horizon. A silence fell over them all. Finnglas gripped the wolf-prow. Even Arthmael was quiet, racing through the depths in front of them.

At last they heard it, above the hissing bow-wave. Morwenna's song rising to the autumn sky. A shining song, like a pearl between rocks of granite, like a blackbird outside a prison, like the song a mother sings by the sick-bed of her child. Arthmael swam faster than ever. The wind moaned in the rigging, and the waves wept against the sides.

Finnglas whirled round.

'She's singing to them! Some of them must still be alive!'
Arthmael leaped away towards the sound of Morwenna's voice, swifter than even the ship could follow him.

18

They caught sight of her at last, curled on a rock at the shore's edge, the iris-blue of her tail a bright blossom in a land of grey. The herd of ponies, smaller now, was huddled on the beach, some standing with drooping heads, some lying down. Morwenna's arm was round the bay mare's neck, resting on weary shoulders, hands stroking the heavy nose, the closed eyes.

Tears were running freely down Finnglas's cheeks as she ran to uncover the hold.

Arthmael came swimming back.

'They've had no rain yet. Even the seaweed is gone. Quick, make a fire on the beach and feed them.'

They splashed ashore and lit a great fire of driftwood. They brought sacks of corn and cooking pots and made a steaming gruel. The horses' nostrils began to twitch. Their heavy heads lifted and turned. Their hooves shuffled nearer. As soon as it was cool enough to bear, Finnglas thrust in her hand. She carried some, cupped in her palm, to the bay mare. The pony opened her eyes wonderingly. A swollen tongue felt its way out between yellowed teeth. She began to lick Finnglas's palm.

The white stallion moved forward.

'You remembered us,' he whinnied. 'The whole world forgot us, but you remembered. How can we thank you?'

They moved among the horses, feeding them all. Finnglas and Niall would not let them eat much at first. When the thrusting, nuzzling lips found no more, the herd moved obediently away and lay down on the beach. Their dark eyes closed in a sleep that would bring life and not death.

And Morwenna sang on, with a song like a rainbow after

storm, like sunshine on ripe harvest, like a candle of thanksgiving.

Finnglas suddenly ran down to the rocks, threw her arms around the mermaid and kissed her. The song broke off in splinters of silver laughter. Morwenna slipped through her arms and dived into the sea to find Arthmael.

Erc had caught fish for the crew. Niall baked bread with the corn and they feasted round the embers of the fire.

That night they slept, exhausted. They did not hear the rain, drumming on the roof of the cabin. The horses twitched their tails in their sleep. They had forgotten the meaning of this beating from the sky.

It was Finnglas who woke first and strode out on to the deck. She looked around her in the sparkling air. The whole island had changed. A fuzz of pale green covered it like a mantle, transforming its appearance, as Finnglas herself had been transformed from stained boots and tunic to scarlet skirt and flowered blouse.

'Wake up!' she shouted, rushing back to the cabin and shaking the others. 'Oh, Arthmael!' she called to the ocean. 'Come quickly! The grass! The grass is growing!'

Arthmael and Morwenna came racing through the waves, leaping from the water, raising their laughing faces to her, his glistening black, hers white, shattering the shallows with their swishing tails.

Pangur came stepping sleepily out on deck and Finnglas seized him, whirling him round above her head.

'Look, Pangur! It's all right! We only have to feed them till the grass is tall, and they will live the winter!'

The horses moved briskly down the beach to greet them.

'You have brought us hope,' the stallion called across the water.

The grass grew swiftly. Before their eyes, the ponies' sides started to swell; their coats began to gleam, their eyes to shine.

When they opened the last sack of corn they held a party. The horses danced for them, cantering a slow pattern on the beach, weaving their nodding manes and rippling tails in shining, twisting, interlacing spirals. And out in the bay, Arthmael and Morwenna wheeled and sang till everyone was giddy.

Niall leaned over the rail and smiled with satisfaction as he watched them.

'That's that, then. The wolves are routed. The horses are fed. We are free to go. We can be home for Christmas.'

'Home!' There was longing in Pangur's voice.

The laughter fell from Finnglas's face. She turned from the horses. Her voice rose dangerously.

'Home? Have you forgotten about Melisant? I haven't found her.'

'Finnglas!' wailed Pangur softly.

'Melisant is dead,' said Niall.

A strange clicking voice spoke below them.

'Haven't you *all* forgotten someone?' the dolphin said sternly.

They turned. Erc stood in the bows with his back to them. He had not joined in their joy. His hands were endlessly knotting and unknotting a piece of rope.

'Erc!' said Niall, striding up to him. 'Erc! I'm sorry! This was all your doing. You risked your life to save us. Me, Finnglas, the horses. And now you have lost your home, and your father's boat as well. Isn't there anything we can do to repay you?'

'No,' said Erc, without looking up.

'But there must be something.'

'It wouldn't be any good. I don't know where she is.'

'Who?'

'My mother. I told you. Jarlath sold her as a slave.'

19

Slowly they turned to look at one another, conscience-stricken.

'Don't you know *anything* about her?' Pangur asked Erc.

He shook his head sadly.

'No one could tell me where the slavers came from. The ship that took her brought gold for Jarlath's palace. For that he sold my mother. They said she was handy with the gutting-knife. Some lord might want her to clean fish or disembowel pigs for his table.'

'There's no shame in that,' said Niall, wiping a knife on his robe. 'It's mackerel for supper.'

'And you've no idea what land the ship came from?' asked Finnglas.

Morwenna floated up to them. Her hair spread round her in the water like an unloosed sheaf of corn.

'Is it news you are wanting?' she asked. 'News of sea-folk that trade in gold and slaves?'

'Do you know?' asked Finnglas, turning sharply. 'Do you know where she is? What king would buy people for gold?'

Morwenna shook her bright head. 'No. But I know where news is to be had. Stories of all that sail or swim or fly the seven seas. I can guide you to where the wild sea-horses gather, from the south and the west and the east. Where the herds go thundering through the islands in the autumn gales. Where the stamping of their hooves and the roaring of their stallions boom from the cliffs to the skies. I can take you to the Great Gate of the Isles, the Dorus Mór, by the whirlpool of Corryvrechan.'

Pangur let out a yell of horror. 'The Corryvrechan! I've heard of that! The Old Woman of Corryvrechan who sucks ships down to the bottom of the sea! I want to go *home*!'

'He's right. We've all heard of it. We can't go there!' cried Niall.

He looked round for support. But Finnglas was on her knees, leaning down to the water eagerly.

'Is it true, Morwenna? Will they come to us from every part of the ocean? Do they see what lives beneath the waves? All of it?'

'All waves must come that way at last, though they circle the oceans. If there is news of the sea, it will be there, at the Great Gate, Dorus Mór.'

'Then they would know . . . if Melisant . . . '

No one spoke. Arthmael swam past. He leaped over a rock, swam a figure of eight underwater, came up balancing a crab on his nose and tossed it into Finnglas's face. She threw it away, but Niall ran after it and picked it up for the cooking pot. Arthmael lay still in the water, looking up at them out of one bright eye.

Niall swallowed. 'Well, we can ask them, can't we? It looks as if we're going there, whatever I say.'

Arthmael leaped straight up out of the sea.'Bravely spoken, Niall! To the south! It is time!'

The grass was blowing on the cliff tops like the waves of an upland sea when they left the horses.

Erc showed them how to skin the hides from three dead ponies and make themselves cloaks and boots and caps against the winter weather. But Finnglas turned away, choking. She stumbled off across the island, searching every cranny, every cave, examining every fallen skeleton for the last time. Not one of them resembled a piebald mare with a long white blaze down her nose. When she came back, Niall held out to her a cloak and boots of jet-black fur. Finnglas shook her head.

'I can't,' she said. 'I just can't.'

Behind her Arthmael's voice clicked. 'Go on, Finnglas. Be a fool again. Pretend that with the warmth of your body you can make one of them live a little longer.'

Finnglas put on the cloak, over the draggled scarlet skirt

and the stained sleeves.

Next morning, there was ice on the rigging. Erc looked north. 'We must go now. The seas are closing.'

The ponies splashed through the breakers, neighing farewell.

The bay mare breathed on Finnglas's face. 'I know what it is to have loved and lost, Finnglas.'

'God speed!' cried the stallion.

'A thousand thanks!'

'May the horses of Manawydan bear you safely!'

The ship leaped away under Erc's hand, as though it felt the ice-floes gathering behind it, teeth sharper than Jarlath's sea-wolves. Each day they appeared without warning, where yesterday there had been open water.

Blue-black the waves, ice-white their crests, and the wind bending the tall mast like a stem of grass. The crew huddled in their fur-lined cloaks. The ship flew south.

The islands of the Hebrides came at them out of the mist like a remembered dream. A great cheer rose from the deck. Land. Britain. But Erc crouched in the bows, peering forward, listening for the roar of the waves at the meeting-place of waters.

One morning, Arthmael and Morwenna had vanished.

'I know where they've gone,' said Pangur wistfully. 'To the holy island of Columcille. To Iona. I expect they're playing with the seal-folk round the rocks where I first found him. I wish he'd taken me with him. I'd rather be on Iona than anywhere . . . except home.'

The wind struck colder. Grey islands rose on either side of them. Silent, mysterious.

'Is it far now?' said Erc.

'I don't know,' Niall told him. 'We've never been here before.'

They were all silent then. Erc came back and took the helm from Finnglas. He made them reef the cracking sail, but still the ship lunged forward, straining at her harness like a half-broken stallion.

Waves crashed on the rocks around them. Pillars of spray

flung higher than Jarlath's tower. Boats, specks in the distance, scurried for the shore. Then flying foam swirled before the bows and the islands were lost.

'Make for the harbour!' bellowed Niall between cupped hands. 'We can't sail in this!'

'What harbour?' shouted Erc. 'We'd wreck her on the rocks. We have to stand off the shore!'

South blindly, madly through the drenching spray. Pangur had taken Erc's place, perched in the bows, tail streaming in the wind, peering slit-eyed through the sea-spume for a sudden rock, for hidden death.

And then they heard it. Deep, chilling, booming, like a great tethered beast in a cavern.

The hungry roar of the whirlpool of Corryvrechan.

20

They felt the sweat break out on them, chilling them instantly. They peered through the flying grey but they could see nothing.

'Where is it? Where is it?' Niall cried anxiously, speaking for all their fears.

But the roar seemed to come from all round them, like thunder in the deeps.

'Why doesn't Arthmael come?' shouted Finnglas. 'Why has he left us alone?'

She gripped the wolf's head. 'To the Great Gate! I command you! Not the whirlpool. The Great Gate!'

Then they heard Pangur scream in terror.

'Help! She's got me! She's pulling me! I can't swim against it!'

'It's Pangur!' cried Finnglas from the bows. 'He's fallen overboard! The Corryvrechan's got him!'

The cat was streaming away from them like a hooked fish on the end of a line. They had a vanishing glimpse of white fur and silvered tail struggling under the green waves.

'Pangur!' yelled Niall helplessly. 'Hold on!'

But the cat had gone.

Erc wrenched at the tiller. The gale blew his ginger hair back from his brow like tongues of fire and under the freckles his sweating face was grey.

'I can't hold the ship!' he gasped. 'She's going sideways! The Old Woman's got us too!'

The ship heeled to the west. The sea was fighting the wind. The waves grew mountainous with anger. The mast creaked dangerously under its shortened canvas and the planks groaned as if they would spring apart. Niall ran to help Erc, but struggle as they would, they could not turn the ship.

Shadows of islands began to fly at them out of the spray, a closing gap, a funnel of rock. Pangur had disappeared completely, his cries swallowed up in the tremendous bellow of the Corryvrechan that filled the grey world. The ship went hurtling after him.

'Arthmael! Arthmael!' shouted Finnglas, her voice tiny in the maelstrom of sound.

'Sing!' commanded Niall, his huge hands uselessly fighting to turn the tiller. 'That is all there is left to us now.'

His chant rose for a moment above the storm like a ragged banner.

> *'I bind unto myself today*
> *The strong name of the Trinity . . .'*

Finnglas joined in the hymn, gasping as the wind snatched the words from her lips.

> *'. . . The flashing of the lightning free,*
> *The whirling wind's tempestuous shocks . . .'*

Pangur shot under their stern.

'There he is!'

Niall bellowed to Finnglas. 'Take off your cloak. Yes, you too, Erc.'

'No! You can't swim for it!' shouted Erc. 'You'll be lost like Pangur. We have to stay with the boat!'

But the monk was busy on the heeling deck, his reddened fingers quickly knotting. Erc watched him grimly and then threw him his cloak.

> *'I bind unto myself today*
> *The power of God to hold and lead . . .'*

'Look! I can see Pangur again! On the port bow!' Finnglas craned dangerously over the wave-swept rail. There was the flash of a white paw and draggled fur.

But even as they crowded to the side they felt the ship turning beneath them, spinning round.

'The whirlpool!' yelled Finnglas. 'The Corryvrechan!'

Pangur flew past them.

'Now!' called Niall, and flung out a skein of pony hides. It soared through the air, in a flash of bay and brown and black, and fell into the waves, flattening them for a moment. In frantic haste they hauled on the sides and like a salmon net the cloaks came scooping in beneath the stern. Niall lifted the shivering cat out of its folds.

But the ship was being whirled faster and faster, corkscrewing. A hole was beginning to open in the sea. A glistening black mouth.

'It's too late!' shouted Erc. 'We're all going to die together. The Old Woman will swallow us and spit out the timbers like kindling.'

Behind him, Niall thundered now to the end of the hymn.

> *'Christ be with me, Christ within me,*
> *Christ behind me, Christ before me.*
> *Christ beside me, Christ to win me,*
> *Christ to comfort and restore me.'*

Black cliffs went flying giddily past in circles. The dark mouth was gaping wider. A funnel of water smooth as polished rock. A hungry throat. The nose of the ship was pulling, dipping, diving, roped like a helpless calf to the force that bellowed in triumph from the bottom of the sea. The stern rising, slithering, toppling.

'Arthmael!' shrieked Finnglas.

A rampart of white water swept across the whirlpool. Stallions neighing higher than the screaming gale. The great, hungry mouth of the sea struggled, narrowed, stretched in a twisted grimace, fought to stay open, closed round a howl of fury. The glassy walls were gone. Trampled, broken, pulped beneath a thousand hooves. The flying herd of sea-horses swept the ship backwards, spun it round, buffeted it, tossed it from one to the other, raced with it, played with it, rushed it towards the cliffs. The rocks flew past them as the horses bucked and reared beneath them, throwing them over their manes, catching them on a shining back, leaping the shoals and despositing them at last, bobbing gently in the blue, bright sunshine of the Hebrides. The horses surged on.

Arthmael appeared, smiling and panting slightly.

'Goodness me! That was exciting, wasn't it? I'm sorry if I left it a little late.' He stood on his tail and looked over the side. 'Is Pangur safe?'

Niall wiped the sweat from his face with a shaking hand. 'That was close! I thought . . . '

The dolphin's eyes met his and twinkled.

'You do me wrong. Have I ever failed to come when you needed me? Your ship has brought you where you wanted to be. You have sailed through the Great Gate, the Dorus Mór.'

At that, Erc ran quickly to the stern and leaned over. All round him, the white horses of the sea were running, from the east and the west, a great herd without numbering, cantering between the islands to their meeting place.

'Fair horses, I bid you tell me! To which country did King Jarlath sell my mother?'

The waves whinnied as they passed him.

'We are not yours to bid. We carry slave-ships and we carry saints. There were many women like the one you speak of.'

'But *where*?' begged Erc. 'For the sound of your voices in the surf, tell me where they have taken her?'

'For that we will speak, and that only. They took her south. To a land where the snow falls late and the spring comes early. Where the pigs grow fat under the apple trees and the rivers teem with salmon. Where the hills yield fairy gold. A winter wind will take you to the Summer Land.'

At the name of Finnglas's home, Niall looked round, startled. But Finnglas, in the bows, had not heard. She dropped to her knees, calling down pleadingly.

'Sweet horses, bright horses, the Princess Finnglas begs you, speak! What news can you tell me of Melisant?'

A gust swept across the sound. The wind fell suddenly. All the wide sea between the islands lay blue and gently 'apping. The white horses had all gone.

The ocean was silent. No one spoke. Then Finnglas gave a great sob.

Niall rested his hand on her shoulder.

'We tried to tell you, Finnglas.'

The dolphin's clown face rose level with hers.

'Why does no one ask *me* about Melisant?'

'Oh, Arthmael! Is it too late? Can't I save her?'

He brushed the tears from her cheeks, leaving them wetter than before.

'You, Finnglas? It is not within your power to undo the past. You cannot dance where I have danced. What *you* have done is done. But what I have undone is undone for ever. And I will share the pain of your doing, if you will share the joy of my Undoing.'

'Does that mean . . .? That I *will* see her again?'

'Trust me, Finnglas. I need all your courage now. And the end of this voyage is the beginning of your journey. Lay your hand on the wolf-head one last time, and bid him find Erc's mother.'

For a long moment his eyes met hers.

They watched her rise. Pale but unquestioning, she reached out her hand to the prow and did as Arthmael bid her.

21

They ran before the winter. The north wind came with long strides down the grey seas behind them. Storms heaped mountainous waves before their path. A lesser ship would have foundered. Icicles hung from the shrouds in the slow, dark dawn, and to breathe the wind was like swallowing sharp swords.

Grey land showed fitfully on the starboard bow. Niall, battered by the icy rain, clung to the rail.

'You know what that is, don't you? The shores of Erin,' he said sorrowfully. 'In the convent, they will be making ready for the feast of Christmas. Brewing ale, baking meats. The door of the guesthouse will stand open to all comers, and a fire will be blazing on the hearth.'

'Go home if you want to,' said Erc through purpled lips. 'This quest is mine alone.'

'We stay together,' said Pangur. 'We owe you more than that.'

Silently he swallowed his homesickness.

'I have no home, either,' Finnglas told him.

They raised their Christmas hymn off the Land's End. At midnight a great school of dolphins rose singing from the sea all around them. Whistling for joy across the frosty sky. Dancing, tumbling, cavorting. Filling the night with laughter and with magic. With a shout of gladness, Arthmael dived away to join them and their welcoming cries of merriment rang to the stars. They left him dancing with the dolphins.

At daybreak they bade farewell to Britain. They passed the Isles of Scilly and the last western rock. The vast ocean stretched before them, joyless, colourless. They seemed to be the only ship upon it, pursued by cloud and darkness and cold. The wind veered bitterly into the east. They fought with storms that raised the waves in tumbling walls. They heard the gale twang the shrouds like bowstrings. They saw their food dwindle and stale. And still the ship sailed on with no sign of turning.

Then there came a day when, in the width of one wave, they seemed to sail out of winter into spring. Above them, the cloud ended, like the line of a grey-brown rampart. In front of them, all was blue as the first violets. The hollows in the waves the purple of heartsease. And the sky above them like a bluebell wood. Gulls flashed across it, unbearably white.

The decks steamed in the sun, and they spread cloaks and sails to dry, and lifted chapped arms and faces to the warmth. Suddenly, for the first time in weeks, Arthmael surfaced in their sparkling wake.

Finnglas was at the helm. They heard her cry out. 'It's Arthmael!'

Next moment, 'The tiller! I can't hold it! The ship is turning!'

Erc leaped to help her. He lifted his face to the sky.

'It's not the wind. But the ship wants to turn. There's no holding her!'

The ropes flapped dangerously. The sail cracked and billowed. The yard-arm crashed across. Niall and Pangur ran amidships, hastening to haul in the sheets. The golden wolf-head came questing round across the wind and turned its hunting muzzle into the north.

With a set face, Arthmael led them, faster than the wind could carry them. He did not look back.

Land was born again out of the sea. Blue, distant hills. They crowded into the bows, watching. Arthmael raced on beneath the surface, silently.

The hills took colour. Woods peopled its slopes, bare branches reddened with buds, beginning to take fire, gold-green with opening leaves.

A broad river opened, a town crowding down to its shores. And crowning the hilltop above it, a fortress, flashing with spears. Finnglas gripped the rail, staring disbelievingly at it.

'No!' she whispered.

The ship was swinging round again, nosing further into the breeze, turning for the shore.

'No,' cried Finnglas. 'No!'

Niall strode across to her. 'Steady, Finnglas.'

There were fishing boats in the harbour, slaves working at the waterside, warriors wrestling in the fields outside the fortress.

Finnglas called desperately, 'It isn't true! I won't believe it! Turn the ship! Quickly, Erc! Turn the ship out to sea!'

'I can't. She doesn't answer to the helm. Don't you see?' His face was shining. 'Don't you see, Finnglas? This is journey's end! My mother's *here*!'

'What's the matter, Finnglas?' asked Pangur. 'Why are you so pale?'

They were both staring at the princess. Niall put his arm round her shoulders.

'Didn't either of you hear the horses? Don't you understand? This is the Summer Land. Where the snow falls late and the spring comes early and the hills are full of gold that kings desire. Journey's end is Kernac's kingdom. It was *Finnglas's father* who bought the slaves from Jarlath.'

With a low cry, Erc turned away. A darkness seemed to deepen on the deck, separating them from one another.

Pangur mewed softly, 'Drusticc's words have come true. *The hearth that is home, and the blood of your belonging.* So *that* was why Arthmael sent us to Jarlath's kingdom!'

'But surely this is good news, isn't it?' said Niall heartily. 'The best news of Erc's mother we could have had. King Kernac will be so happy to see his daughter back from the dead, he'll give her anything she wants. Finnglas could ask him for the freedom of a hundred slaves!'

'And you think that makes it all right?' Erc asked bitterly. 'The king's property. To keep, or give away. Ranvaig, my mother, a woman that was free?'

'I didn't know!' protested Finnglas. 'We always had slaves. But I didn't know he bought and sold them. People, for gold!'

'Did you never think to ask?' said Erc.

They glared at each other.

'Look out!' cried Pangur suddenly, springing towards the tiller. 'The fishing fleet! We're running them down!'

Shouting and cursing broke out beneath the bows. All round them the water was crowded with small leather boats, bobbing wildly, trying to back away from their prow. Lean, brown fishermen leaped for the oars, hauled on the nets. Silver knives were flashing, ropes flying, silver fish leaping away, the surface of the water dancing madly over the escaping shoal.

Arthmael jumped over a wave as the fish raced past him. One of the fishermen raised his arm and pointed.

'The sea-devil! The scarred dolphin! The king has set a price of gold on his head.'

At once there was tumult in the fishing fleet. Knives flashed upwards in the sunshine. A fish spear whistled through the air and plunged into the waves.

'Arthmael!' shrieked Pangur in horror.

The dolphin leaped into the air and dived. A shadow raced under the surface, blue-black as the hollows beneath the mountain, streaking for the open sea.

The curraghs were spinning round, nets dropping overboard, oars driving through the sparkling waves, men straining as they rowed, the steersmen yelling.

'The dancing dolphin! The breaker of nets! The friend of murderers! Spear him! Spear him!'

'Arthmael! Swim!' screamed Pangur.

The sun dazzled the water beyond the harbour. The wide, open sea lay empty. The leaping curraghs faltered.

'It's all right! He's got away!' cried Pangur, flinging himself round Niall's neck.

'Pray God he never comes back,' muttered Niall. 'King Kernac is Arthmael's enemy. We killed his son, and Arthmael set us free.'

'Can't we turn round and go?'

Niall looked at Erc. 'Not till we have found the slaves and set Erc's mother free.'

A curragh was putting out from the shore, heading towards them. Erc, his face still set and angry, threw the anchor overboard.

Niall and Pangur hurried to run down the sail. Only Finnglas stood shocked and unmoving, looking up at her father's palace on the hill where she had not wished to come ever again.

The curragh was nearing. Warriors stood poised in the bows, hands on swords, their long hair pulled by the wind, moustaches bristling.

'My father's men. I know them,' murmured Finnglas.

She moved proudly forward to stand before the wolf-prow. The others let her pass.

The boat bumped the side. Scarred knuckles gripped the rail. A black-whiskered warrior vaulted on board and whipped the sword from his scabbard with an oath. In an instant, twenty more swarmed over the side. Pangur dived into the coil of rope, out of sight.

'Unfriendly is Jarlath's wolf-ship! Do the wolves of the North come to trade or to steal? You have cut our nets and robbed the king of his catch. You shall pay dearly to the fisherfolk of Kernac.'

'Tomméné,' called Finnglas, facing him. 'Don't you see who I am?'

He brushed her aside as if she had been a horsefly.

Erc stood his ground in front of the warrior. 'I'm sorry. I'm a fisherman too. I should have known better than the others.'

Finnglas stamped her foot. 'Tomméné!'

'Bring out your unlucky captain. Does the coward hide from our swords?'

Finnglas's voice rang out behind him.

'I command this ship. Look, Tomméné mac Ruain! By those hands which first lifted me on to a horse. Look once again on Finnglas, your princess.'

He whirled round then, his face purple as a thundercloud. His sword flashed out, stabbing her breast like a heron's beak.

'Have a care what you say!' he shouted. 'That name has not been spoken here for three long years. Two names we may not breathe on pain of death. The princess and her brother.' His eyes flew up to the palace on the hill. 'Deep is the king's grief, as a bottomless well. Wild is the rage of Kernac. We are a people that tread softly and in fear.'

Finnglas had turned white, with the sword-point buried in her bodice. But she did not flinch.

'Tomméné. I am *alive*. Don't you recognize me?'

She stood erect before him. Three years had passed since she had ridden her pony into the sea and disappeared. She was taller now, more womanly. The salt-caked black fur cloak swung back from the dress in which Jarlath had clothed her for her wedding-day. But the scarlet skirt was stained and grubby, the embroidered blouse torn. Her brown hair tangled loose below her shoulders.

Tomméné stared at her savagely. Then a smile split his whiskered face. The sword-point dropped and his huge hand caressed her arm.

'I have lost count of the pretty women I have known, from the burning sands of Morocco to icy Thule. What is one more? It is not your faces I remember!'

Finnglas's hand flew to her hip, where once her sword had hung.

'By heaven, you insult me, Tomméné! Take me to my father!'

But the warrior's eyes had fallen on Niall. They narrowed suddenly. At once every trace of a smile vanished from his face.

'A *monk*, is it? A Christian priest on Jarlath's ship! What trickery is this?' He spun round suspiciously. 'How came you three by this ship? Where is Jarlath's captain? What have you done with the wolf-crew?'

Now twenty swords were raised, blades ringing Niall round. Finnglas's voice rose loud in anger.

'Release that monk! Kernac's daughter commands you. This ship was the gift of Arthmael.'

Tomméné turned on her with a roar.

'Hold your whining, strumpet! It was a monk that killed our prince. A monk and a cursed white cat. The princess met her death riding into the sea for vengeance on them. Since then it has been cruel winter in the Summer Land. I shall take the priest where we take all unwelcome strangers. To the slave-pens. If he lives till morning, he will find himself in the darkness of the mines, digging Kernac's gold. But dressed as a monk, I do not think he will reach them alive. Either way, he will not see the sun again.'

Pangur crouched lower in the coil of rope and curled himself up as small as possible.

Erc protested. 'If you want a workman, take me! Shall I go free while my mother is a slave?'

'Tomméné mac Ruain!' Finnglas cried in despair. '*Look at me!*'

93

'Hold your peace! Seize them all three, and take them to the slave-market!'

Pangur trembled in his coil of rope. He heard cries and the bump of feet against the sides as the three captives were bundled into the boat. The creak of oars rowed them towards the town.

Pangur was left alone. Shivering with fright, he peeped out of his hiding-place. He was terrified of being seen on the deck. A monk and a white cat. He was in Kernac's town, and they *knew* he had killed the king's son.

The fleet had rowed back into harbour, muttering angrily. All round him the fishing boats were hauling in their broken nets. The air was loud with oaths. But worse than that was happening on shore.

The cat crept out of his hiding-place. He gave a sudden start. A lone sentry was leaning over the wolf-prow. But the guard had his back to Pangur. No one was watching the deck.

The sea sucked against the sides, green, cloudy, cold. Pangur swallowed. With a great gulp of air, he dived overboard.

23

The chill water snatched his breath away. The green depths were bubbling past. But he could not breathe in water. His lungs were bursting.

He broke surface in the middle of the fishing fleet. He gasped with terror and plunged out of sight again. A clouded darkness now, beneath the boats. Under the shouting, deep silence.

A fishing net rose suddenly in front of his face.

'Arthmael!' he mewed soundlessly. He backed away, terrified of entanglement.

But even as he called, he knew that Arthmael must never come here.

Then his paws felt a surface beneath them. Smooth and strong as a rock. All at once something was lifting him up, thrusting him through the water. He squawked with alarm and swallowed a mouthful of brine.

'Hold tight!' The laughter bubbled up from beneath him.

'Arthmael!' he mouthed. And then, 'You shouldn't be here!'

'Don't try to talk underwater,' chuckled the dolphin. 'I need you alive, not drowned.'

Next moment he was flung backwards, so that he had to dig his claws into the slippery back to stop himself from falling off. He felt himself being rushed along at a tremendous speed. He could only cling on tightly, aware he must be hurting the dolphin, yet knowing that Arthmael would bear the pain joyfully. Shadows raced overhead as they streaked away from the fishing fleet.

The water flashed past, green, brown, golden. They surfaced on a quiet beach. They were on the other side of the hill away from the harbour. The side of the palace ramparts showed above the trees.

Pangur tumbled off on to the sand. He spat out a mouthful of sea-water and gulped salt air.

'You shouldn't have come, Arthmael!' he gasped.'Kernac's people would kill you if they could.'

The dolphin lay in the shadows, smiling mischievously. 'Then they are the ones who most need our help.'

'It's not them! It's Niall and Finnglas and Erc. They've been taken prisoner.'

'I know. Good luck.'

'Good luck? Why, where am I going?'

'To Kernac's palace, of course. To set them free and rescue Erc's mother.'

'But I can't! Not all by myself!'

'You have raced with the Dolphin, Pangur. You have ridden the wild sea-horses of Manawydan. You'll think of something.'

'But I'm only a very small cat.'

The dolphin's eyes twinkled kindly. 'And a very brave one.'

Pangur's nose blushed. He shut his eyes tight, then opened them very wide.

'All right!' he gasped. 'I'll try, if you say I can!'

He took one last look at the dolphin's loving smile. Then, without giving himself time to change his mind, he turned and ran up the hill into the trees.

The wood ended suddenly in sunlight. A road skirted the field below the ramparts of Kernac's dun. Pangur stepped out of the grass.

A moment later he flung himself back under the bushes and crouched trembling.

'Someone's coming! Donkeys. No! Humans!'

Out of the oak trees came a struggling procession. Men and women, bent almost on all fours under the mound of firewood on their shoulders. They stumbled down the path. Beside them strode a single upright figure. Pangur heard a whip crack and a feeble cry. One of the mounds of firewood fell in a heap, with a ragged form beneath it. Again the whip cracked. The mound twitched and lay still. The procession trudged past it.

'Slaves,' whispered Pangur. 'Like Erc's mother.'

In through the gates. Behind Kernac's palace stretched a line of thatched huts. As the slaves disappeared, fresh smoke rose thickly from the roofs. It bore an unmistakable smell of fish.

Pangur raised his head and sniffed hungrily.

'King Kernac feasts well tonight. No wonder the fishermen were angry to lose their catch.'

The slaves stumbled out through the gate again, their firewood unloaded. They shuffled back towards the forest. The path was empty.

Pangur took a deep breath and sprinted across it into the long grass. There were warriors at Kernac's gate. He had a glimpse beyond it. Two mastiffs ranged the yard, growling. The white cat felt the hair on his back crawl coldly. He crept round to the back of the ramparts and sprang on to the wall.

Sheds opened on the sunlight of the kitchen yard. He whisked into the nearest one and crouched in a corner, his eyes widening in the gloom. The slaves toiled in silence. Men fed the fires, while women worked at long, trestle tables, heaving fish from baskets, splitting them open, gutting them, throwing the entrails aside, lifting, gutting, tossing, till their arms were weary and the floor grew slippery with blood and slime. Pangur crept in among them, searching their faces. Brown, freckled, rosy, from many lands they came, working in a tired, frightened silence. Feet kicked him aside. But one pair of hands bent and snatched him to safety.

'What are you doing here, little visitor? This is no place for you. In Kernac's palace they say white cats are unlucky.' She set him down and pushed back her grey hair.

'But we're all unlucky here. To lose a husband, and then a home and son. Here!'

She pushed a fat salmon roe quickly off the edge of the table. Pangur tore his eyes away from it, though the saliva was running down his jaws. He looked up at her swiftly.

97

'That home you lost,' he said. 'Was it in Jarlath's kingdom? Are you Erc's mother?'

She gasped. But a shadow darkened the door. The slave-master strode in.

'Are you not finished yet? Where are those salmon? The king banquets tonight. Hurry, you daughters of pigs!'

The fallen roe was just out of Pangur's reach. It lay in the sunlight, soft, pink, moist. His whole body ached with hunger. If only the man would go. The slave-master turned. And his eyes fell on it too. He roared with rage.

'What waste is this! You careless sow!' The whip cracked across the woman's shoulders and she screamed. Behind her back Pangur darted for the door, carrying his grumbling stomach into the open air.

He fled through the gate, under the startled noses of the mastiffs, and stopped short. A shouting, angry crowd was coming up the path from the town. In front strode Finnglas, bound like a prisoner, but her head held high, staring round her unbelievingly, still waiting for someone, somewhere, to recognize her. Niall's cowl was drawn around his ears, his head ducked as stones came shying round his shoulders. Only Erc thought nothing about himself, his eyes searching, searching for one face in this foreign land that would not be a stranger.

'The monk! Death to the monk!'

'People of the Summer Land!' shouted Finnglas. 'Don't you know who I am?'

'Pirates! They stole King Jarlath's golden ship.'

'Thieves!'

'They broke our nets and lost our catch!'

'Robbers!'

'To the slave-pens!'

'Look at your princess! I am Finnglas!'

A stone, aimed at Niall, struck her on the side of the head. The blood spurted out. At the sight of it the crowd roared with delight.

'It is Finnglas! Finnglas, that you see before you!'

Only Pangur could save them now. With a loud 'Miaow!'

he threw himself across the path in front of them.

And the crowd saw him.

'It's the white cat! The cursed white cat! The Unlucky One!'

'The prince's killer! Murderer! After him!'

The stones that had been gathered for Niall pelted now over Pangur's head. The guards were running from the gate. With a whisk of his white tail Pangur bolted straight into the crowd through Finnglas's legs.

'Erc!' he yelled as he flew past the boy. 'The kitchens! Your mother's in there!'

24

Pandemonium broke out. For a moment the crowd had lost him under Finnglas's skirts. He tore through their legs, claws scratching their bare feet, and out on the other side. He wanted to dive into the undergrowth, to be lost to sight. But they must all see him. They must see a small white cat streaking away from the palace. They must forget their prisoners and turn upon him.

'*Miaow*!'

Over the last bare feet like the roots of a forest.

'*Miaow*!'

The crowd turning behind him like the changing tide.

'*Miaow*!'

A fresh roar of fury echoed to the sky.

They had seen him go.

He was running now too fast to look behind. Spurning the soft grass, taking the stony way, the thorny way, making the barefoot crowd shout with anger and pain as they rushed after him. But the warriors were booted and strong. He could hear their feet pounding up the path behind him. Stones were crashing into the bushes all around him. The trees were ahead.

And out of the forest came the column of slaves carrying more firewood, eyes lowered, backs bent, feet plodding everlastingly on. Full tilt he ran towards them, under their ankles, with the warriors storming after him and all the mob pressing behind like flood-water in full spate. Shouts, screams, a tumble of falling bodies. Billets of wood went flying through the air. The slave-drivers were running forward, bellowing, cursing, lashing their whips, fighting with the warriors who were struggling to get past the slaves. Pangur bolted into the trees.

He had one glimpse of Finnglas, Niall and Erc racing for the unguarded gate and the palace beyond. Finnglas was shouting,

'*Father*! I've come back! Father! It's Finnglas!'

A wave of triumph soared through Pangur Bán. He had done it, and he alone! He had saved them all. He had found Erc's mother, and set the prisoners free. With a loud yowl of joy he turned, leaping with great springing strides back to the palace. He bounded on to the ramparts above the kitchens.

'Erc!' he yelled down into the yard. 'This way!'

He landed in front of the doorway. The huge slave-master blocked the way, yelling with rage, and struck out with his whip. But Pangur was too fast for him. He whisked into the kitchen. Under the tables, knocking away the trestles, overturning the baskets of slippery fish-guts. He leaped for the chest of an old man feeding the furnace, and the glowing sticks scattered over the floor. A nest of flames wriggled in the scattered sawdust, hatched into golden snakes, slithering up the walls, and as Pangur shot from the far door, a dragon of fire burst from one thatched roof and leaped for the next.

The palace was in an uproar. Pangur poked his head round the corner of a blazing hut. Slaves, slave-masters, warriors were running for their lives. The milling, shrieking crowd was charging back from the forest. Finnglas, Niall and Erc, their hands still bound, raced round the corner. A grey-haired woman stumbled from a burning doorway. With a cry, Pangur leaped to the roof above her head.

'Erc! Here!'

As the flames charged him, he sprang to the ground.

All round the palace the slaves were scattering, fleeing across the hillside towards the forest and freedom. The crack of the slave-masters' whips was lost in the roar of the flames. A terrible stench of burning fish fouled the air.

The woman stood stock still as the red-haired boy came racing towards her, her face scorched, her hands clasped together, as she wrinkled her eyes against the sun.

'Erc?' she said wonderingly. 'Is it *Erc*?'

A last, satisfied smile curved across Pangur's face.

Erc sprang across the open space and reached out towards her.

'Show me your wrists,' she said grimly. And with a slash of her gutting knife she cut them free.

They were all running for the gate. The palace had taken fire. The nobles rushed into the courtyard, rich chequered cloaks flying behind them. A great red-bearded man burst out of the door waving a huge sword. His cloak held the seven colours that only a king may wear.

'*Father*!' shouted Finnglas, hurling herself in front of him.

'Out of my way, girl! The palace is burning.' He threw her aside.

'Father! It's Finnglas! Don't you recognize me?'

'Would you bar the king's way?' he roared. The flat of his sword knocked her to her knees.

'Father!' yelled Finnglas, reaching out to him.

The king rushed past her furiously. The shouting nobles were bearing down on her. Niall snatched her to her feet. They started to run. Erc pulled his mother behind him. The panic-stricken crowd was sweeping them towards the gate.

There was a rending roar. The roof of the palace was a mass of flames. In front of them the great ridge beam cracked, broke, caved, rolled, tumbled, crashed to the ground in an avalanche of blazing straw.

With a scream, the crowd sprang back. Then the noise hushed into a fearful silence as they stared. Pinned under the beam sprawled the broken body of the king.

25

Finnglas hurled herself forward. Spears flew up, barring her way. Desperately Kernac's nobles pulled the burning thatch away with their bare hands. They wrestled like slaves to raise the blackened beam and lift it clear.

The king lay motionless. The red beard was singed. The chequered cloak charred and torn. He stirred and groaned. Gently, yet not tenderly enough, they turned him over and he groaned again. His face was scorched by the fire.

'Father!' cried Finnglas. But the spears forced her back.

Dubhthac the Druid knelt by the king's side. Kernac grasped his sleeve.

'Listen,' he whispered. 'Can you hear the singing?'

The crowd fell hushed. There was only the crackle of the flames.

'My hurt is mortal. From the Land of the Ever-Young across the sea the voices are calling me. Carry me to the shore.'

'No!' cried Finnglas, from the crowd.

But he could not hear her.

The nobles looked at each other uneasily.

Then Tomméné said roughly, 'It is the king's last command. Do as he says.'

They lifted Kernac on a bed of spears and covered it with his cloak. The songs of the women shrilled in a sharp lament as the warriors carried their wounded king down to the beach.

Still Finnglas struggled to reach him. But they would not let her through.

'What about *us*?' murmured Pangur nervously.

Niall picked up the cat and tucked him under one arm. 'We promised to follow Finnglas. I won't desert her now.'

And he strode on down the hill.

They laid the king on the stones beside the tide-mark. The keening died. A little breeze stirred his charred hair. The blue eyes opened.

'Listen!' He gripped Dubhthac's arm. 'It is coming nearer.'

And then they heard it. A high, strange music far out to sea. In fearful silence they listened as the song came floating towards the harbour on the tide. It passed inside the headland and became a cheerful whistle bobbing between the fishing boats. Niall caught his breath and dropped Pangur on the sand.

A sleek black shape swam round the nearest curragh. Arthmael the Dolphin stood up on his tail, dark-backed against the sun. The fire reddened the long scars down his side. But he was singing still, a wobbling, carolling, laughter-laden song.

The crowd shouted with anger.

'Spear him!' cried Rohan of the Chariots.

The king's brother, Manach, swept out his sword.

'Sea-devil! You freed the murderers of the king's son and took his daughter away. Do you come back now to mock the father's death?'

'No,' smiled Arthmael. Then he shouted in a voice not comical but fearful now, 'Kernac! It is for you I have come. I have brought you what you most desire. Behold your daughter!'

Tomméné whirled round, white-faced. There was a flash of steel as the spears burst apart. In a scurry of stones Finnglas ran across the beach.

'It *was* you!' gasped Tomméné.

She knelt before Kernac. He stared up into her face. Long the king looked at his lost daughter.

'Finnglas?' his voice came hoarsely. 'Is it really you at last?'

'Yes.' The tears were coursing down her cheeks. 'Oh, Father, forgive me. I have stayed away from you too long. I was so angry when you burned the abbey. But that anger has caused the loss of many lives. I should have come home sooner and healed your grief.'

104

The king strove to raise his hand and touch Finnglas's face.

'Finnglas Red-Hand they called you when you rode away. But no more. You have come back to us a woman now.'

He grasped her hand feebly. 'My sword is gone. It will shed blood no more. I am dying, Finnglas.'

'No, Father,' wept Finnglas.'Stay with me.'

From the sea, Arthmael thundered, 'Niall! Pangur Bán!'

Trembling, Niall and Pangur stepped out on to the open beach. Niall fell on his knees in front of the king.

'Forgive me! I slew your son. In a moment's foolish anger I meant to kill Pangur. It was your son who took that blow.'

'It was all my fault,' mewed Pangur. 'I did Niall a great wrong.'

There was a roar of hate from every throat in the crowd, a hiss of steel as every sword was drawn, every spear aimed. Kernac's hand clenched on a stone beside him. His eyes burned like twin blue flames.

Through the tense silence the waves lapped at the tideline.

'Kernac!' sang Arthmael. 'The tide is turning.'

'Forgive them,' begged Finnglas. 'They have saved my life many times over. And much more than my life.'

The king gasped with pain. 'Then that must content my son's honour, who loved you more than his life. Give me your hand, monk. It is the living who will need friends now. When Finnglas is queen, swear that you will guard her till the kingdom is strong.'

'With all my heart,' promised Niall. 'As long as Finnglas needs me, I will stay by her side.'

'And I,' swore Pangur Bán. 'If I'm any use.'

'Father!' pleaded Finnglas.'You mustn't die!'

'Kernac!' sang Arthmael again. 'The tide is falling.'

Kernac looked past her, at the wildly staring ring of faces. He struggled to lift her hand above his head.

'Look on her, all of you. Behold my daughter, Finnglas. I name her *Tanist*. Finnglas shall be my heir.'

'No, Father. No! Don't leave me yet!'

'Honour her now. Swear that you will choose her for your queen. She has the royal blood.'

There was a deep murmur from the nobles.

Through tears that sparkled in the firelight, Finnglas looked round at all their whiskered faces. Tomméné, who had first lifted her on to Melisant, and saw her ride her pony into the sea. Her uncle Manach, who had taught her to wield the sword she had lost. Young Rohan of the Bright Chariots, who could balance on the yoke-pole of a galloping team. Laidcenn the royal harper, who had sung her the legends of the Summer Isle. And Dubhthac the Chief Druid, of the Golden Knife.

Every one of them was a full-grown man. Every one of them was of the royal blood. Every one of them might have hoped to be chosen king. Their hands gripped their sword hilts. Their eyes were flashing. Niall and Erc sprang to stand beside Finnglas.

The swords swept upwards, the flames of the palace blazing in the bright blades. There was a gasp of fear from the crowd.

The nobles grasped the swords by their points. They lowered the hilts to the ground before Finnglas. The hair of their heads swept the stones as they bowed in homage.

'Finnglas is Kernac's heir.'

'Finnglas *Tanist!*'

'Our Queen shall be Finnglas of the Horses!'

'Finnglas of the Horses! Finnglas of the Horses!' The people took up the shout.

Finnglas touched the hilts and gave back the swords.

'I thank you,' she said with difficulty. 'When the time comes, I shall rule you with honour, as Arthmael rules me.'

Then she turned away and cradled the king's head in her arms.

'Kernac!' called Arthmael, turning towards the sea.

'No! Stay, Father, one moment more,' cried Finnglas. She seized the fisher-boy by the hand. 'This is Erc, who rescued all of us and brought us here. Listen to him.'

'Let him ask of me whatever he will. But let him ask it quickly.'

The boy's eyes flashed proudly. 'There is only one thing I want. And it is not a gift I should have had to beg. The freedom of my mother, whom you took as a slave.'

'Let her stand before me . . . So, what is your name?'

'Ranvaig, that was Trian's daughter and Big Erc's wife.'

'You have a noble son. It is not fitting his mother should be a slave.' Through his pain, his mouth twisted in a crooked smile, Kernac spoke. 'Ranvaig, Trian's daughter. I give you your freedom. But with my last breath I take it from you again. I charge you, when I am dead, be to my daughter as the mother she lost.'

'You did not need to ask that,' Ranvaig told him sternly. 'And you should not be talking now.'

The king's eyes sparkled. 'When this tide has ebbed, you shall have all the silence you want.'

'Come, Kernac. The tide is going out,' whistled Arthmael. 'It is time for us to be going too.'

And the dolphin began to swim through the fishing fleet, singing gaily.

'No!' whispered Finnglas.

But the whistle was passing out between the headlands, soaring to the sky. They heard it pass across the sea and die away. The beach was silent. The flames of the palace growled, crackled, spat, flickered, died. In the king's blue eyes the fire of life sprang up for the last time and went out for ever.

Dubhthac the Druid bent over the still form. He passed his golden knife across Kernac's face. Then he stood up and called to the crowd.

'Your king breathes no more. His soul is sped to the Isles of the Ever-Young.'

There was a moment's silence. Then a wailing broke from the women in the crowd.

'Ochone! Ochone!
The soul of our king is fled from us.
Who shall ride before us into battle?
The people of the Summer Land are leaderless.'

And an answering roar from the men rang across the hillside, echoed to the sky, thundered out over the sea.

'Finnglas! Finnglas of the Horses! Finnglas shall be our Queen!'

26

They laid the king's body in a small chapel by the sea. Finnglas knelt at the foot of her father's bier. In the four corners of the room, Niall, Pangur, Erc and his mother Ranvaig watched with her through the long hours of darkness.

At the dead of night there came a footstep at the door. Tomméné rested his hand on Finnglas's shoulder.

'It is midnight, my lady. Let me stand vigil for you for this one hour.'

Finnglas climbed stiffly to her feet.

'For one hour only. You served him loyally in life, Tomméné. Honour him now in death.'

Her friends rose from the shadows and followed her outside.

The embers of the palace still glowed on the hilltop. But Finnglas turned away from it, walking through the damp grass down to the beach.

'Arthmael,' she called quietly.

There was a swishing in the shallows, then a listening silence. They saw nothing in the black waves, but they knew the dolphin had come back.

'Arthmael. I do not want to be queen. I want my father back.'

A head rose in the starlight. The dolphin's voice was unsteady, hovering between love and laughter.

'You see how it feels? Did you ever ask if I wanted to be *your* king? You are a troublesome people to govern!'

'But I cannot rule my father's kingdom. I cannot hold the quarrelling clans apart. I cannot lead them into battle!'

'Do not ask me for a task that is equal to your strength. Ask for my strength that is equal to any task. When you were in trouble, you called to me and I danced for you. I am dancing still. The world is calling you into the dance now, Finnglas, and your people are watching.'

'Then, is there no way out? My father is gone, and I must bear this burden for ever?'

Arthmael whisked up on his tail, all the great length of him shimmering under the stars. He kissed her cheeks, teasing her.

'For ever, is it, Finnglas? How long do you think a human life is? The end will come sooner than you think! Be brave. Take up your burden now, and I will lift it from you in the great Undoing. Then you and your father shall take hands in the dance that knows no end. Trust me. Look there, how I seal my promise!'

And with a chuckle he vanished into the wide sea. A little wave lapped around their feet.

'What did he mean?' Pangur started to say.

Then a drumming began to roll along the beach. The sand began to quiver under their feet. A great cloud of spray was rushing towards them.

'What's that!' cried Pangur, backing away.

The thunder in their ears grew louder and louder. The exploding spray was blotting out the stars.

'Finnglas! Look out!' cried Niall.

But Finnglas took a step forward into the water, hands clasped in front of her, staring breathlessly. Bearing down on her was a whirlwind of darkness. On either side great waves swept to the sky. The night broke apart in avalanches of silver. The whole world pulsed with the beat of surging hooves. And in the heart of the galloping darkness, a long white blaze shone on a velvet nose.

'*Melisant*!' shouted Finnglas. 'It's Melisant! She's *alive*!'

The charging horse neighed as it swept past her, striking a thousand chimes from the stars above. The wave engulfed Finnglas.

As the sea fell back, rocking wildly, the others rushed fearfully to the water's edge. But Finnglas stood in the surf, drenched and laughing.

110

'Did you see her? Did you see her, Niall, Pangur? She's alive! She's so alive!'

'Too alive!' said Pangur, scrambling away as the pony whirled round at the end of the beach in a scatter of spume. She came storming back towards them, tossing her mane.

'And more than happy,' cried Niall. 'Look at her! She is happiness itself.'

They felt the shock of her passing, heard her glad shout of welcome, saw her tail stream out behind her spangled with stars. They watched her enviously. Before the fierce swiftness of her galloping, their living feet felt like lumps of clay.

'And to think that when I found her I was going to ask her to forgive me!' laughed Finnglas. 'You can *feel* her joy. We are the ones to be pitied.'

For the third time Melisant raced past them. And she threw back her head till the mountains rang with her neighing. As she flung the waves apart, the slopes of the night burst into silver blossom like a dark wood waking to the first springtime. The spume sped sparkling in her wake all the way to the far end of the beach.

Far out in the deep a fluting whistle called. They heard her hooves drumming on over the sand, a faint splashing followed, then a deep silence.

For a long time they stood without speaking, like people who do not want to wake from a dream. The spray seemed to have tangled in Finnglas's lashes. The starlight glittered in her eyes.

Ranvaig, Erc's mother, spoke gently.

'You have left your father childless, before his burial. This is the day of his last voyage, and the day of your Choosing.'

Finnglas pulled her dripping cloak around her and stepped on to the sand.

'You are right. I did not honour him enough while he lived. I owe him this last love, to kneel at his feet for this one night. But a morning will come when we shall be together for ever. Watch with me, all of you. I have much need of friends.'

'This we have promised,' said Niall.

'We have lost our own home. We are your people now,' said Erc.

'We are Finnglas's friends,' Pangur told him. 'But *Arthmael's* people.'

'It is well spoken, little cat,' Finnglas smiled.

She bent down and rubbed his ears.

The spray sang. Waves chased their feet. The sea was rocking with the echoes of a great laughter.